I0598980

Spots Before Marriage

Love's Infestation Series #2

May your life be a story in faithful living

Sophie Dawson

~~~~~

©2017 Sophie Dawson
ISBN: 978-1-63376-016-5

This is a work of fiction. Names, characters, businesses, places, events and incidents are either the products of the author's imagination or used in a fictitious manner. Any resemblance to actual persons, living or dead, or actual events is purely coincidental.

Chapter 1

Keith Austin looked up from the sandwich he was struggling to keep together. It seemed to be too full of meat, cheese, and veggies. His eyes widened at what was coming toward him in leaps and barks. A mass of tumbling spotted puppies, all dragging leashes, yipped and barked, eyes seemingly glued to his lunch.

Then they were on him. There hadn't been time to get to his feet, let alone move out of their path. Keith couldn't tell how many there were. All he could tell is that there was a roiling mass of white with black spots all nipping, trying to get to the roast beef he clutched in his hands.

"Down! Get down. Sit." Keith didn't know if it was the words that did it or his tone, but several of the puppies plopped their bottoms down on the grass, the park bench or his shoes. That his feet were in them didn't seem to matter to the puppies.

Deciding that the sandwich was better left to the dogs, he began tearing bits off and feeding them to the ones who were sitting. Soon all the puppies were quiet, poised around the bench hoping for another bite. He counted. Stunned at the final count of fourteen Dalmatian puppies.

"How'd you do that?" A woman's voice called across the lawn. Keith looked from the dogs to her limping toward him. She was petite, not so much in height although she wasn't overly tall. Instead, the young woman was small boned and thin, nearly frail looking. That her knees were skinned and bleeding definitely added to her fragility.

"You're hurt."

The statement was met with a look that said, 'obviously.'

"These all yours?" He waved a hand at the puppies who all jumped up and began dancing around, yipping and biting at each other. "Sit," Keith ordered. It didn't work as well this time. They seemed to know he didn't have any more food he was willing to give them.

Both he and the young woman began grabbing the leashes for each of the dogs. It took a while, but they managed to get a hold of them all before any of the puppies ran off.

"Come on," Keith said. "I've got a first aid kit in my car."

"You carry a first aid kit? I'm surprised. Most guys wouldn't think of it." They began the trek across the grass to the parking lot.

"Hazard of the profession. I'm a doctor. Keith Austin. I'd shake your hand, but mine and yours are full." He lifted the leashes a bit.

"Whitney Houston, and don't say it. My folks were huge fans. They were delighted with a girl after three boys. They're all married. I have five nephews and four nieces. None live here in town now. That's how I ended up with the spotted horde." She waved a hand indicating the puppies. "Evan got transferred and left his females with me. They were both expecting. He was supposed to come and get them. Obviously, he hasn't. I'm not a dog person and not likely to become one after all that's gone on with sixteen dogs, fourteen of which are puppies that need a lot of training. You want one? I'm selling them way under value. They're AKC registered. Or will be when they get a bit older. I was told I couldn't get rid of them until they're at least eight weeks old. They're just past seven."

"Um, no thanks. I'm gone too much to have a puppy or dog. Demanding job and all that." Keith looked around as they approached his car. He really didn't want the puppies jumping on it and scratching the paint. It was a classic that he kept in pristine condition.

The red 1967 Austin Healey Mark III was a treasured possession. Not as much now as before he became a believer in Jesus Christ, but he still liked it and didn't want it damaged by a bunch of unruly spotted dogs.

There was a lamp post nearby, so Keith went to it and looped the leashes around it, knotting them together. Whitney had followed, so he took the ones she held and did the same. He noted that her hands were bleeding as well as her legs.

"You did a number on your knees and palms, there," he said as they left the puppies jumping on each other and tangling the leashes.

Whitney looked down at her damaged appendages. "Yeah, I don't think I should have tried to take them all for a walk at the same time. They're rather small individually, but put them all together, and it's a lot of dog. They sort of took me for the walk and when they began to run — well, I just couldn't keep up. I wanted to get the work over with all at once instead of taking it, like, three times. It ruins several hours if I do that.

"I wanted to have some part of my Saturday not dealing with the dogs. Say, maybe spend some time with my cat, or I don't know. Just doing something that doesn't have to do with work or dogs. It's times like this I really hate Evan, that's the brother who left me with his pregnant dogs.

"I suppose I could just crate them up and ship them to him, but it's really too far and would take too long so they'd suffer. I'm sure not going to give him any of the money I get for selling the beasts. And I'm going to sell all of them or give them away. He's not even getting Betsy and Jewels back. They are going, too. He can come and get them if he wants, all of them, but I don't think he's going to. He won't answer my texts or phone calls now. Hasn't since I let him know the ladies had fourteen puppies. I think he's afraid of me. He should be. I have a nail gun. Several in fact."

They'd moved to his car as she spoke. Keith unlocked the trunk and took out his first aid kit.

Whitney started laughing. "A Pinky and the Brain lunch box is your first aid kit?" She sat on the passenger seat when he opened the car door.

"Hey, it was a great cartoon. I watched it all the

time as a kid. This box is a classic. Besides, it holds everything quite well." Keith opened the box and took out what he needed to treat her injuries. "So, you have nail guns? Any particular reason?" He asked as he began cleaning her palms with wipes.

"I'm a handyperson, Handigirl At Your Service. That's my business. I do just about any sort of work you might need. I'm a licensed electrician and plumber. I'm a pretty mean carpenter. Make a good living at it.

"Most men won't do the small jobs people need done. They want the big remodel or new construction. I can and am willing to take on small projects.

"You know the type. Re-caulk a sink, shower or tub. Replace a toilet or window or ceiling fan. Blow insulation in an attic. Repair just about anything around a house. You name it I've probably done it.

"Some jobs I hire a high school kid to help with the lifting but most things I can do myself. My size can be a handicap or an asset. I might not be as strong as a man, but I fit into small spaces better than most of them can."

As she talked, Keith treated and bandaged her hands and knees. Dried blood still trailed down her legs, but he'd gotten the bleeding stopped.

"That's all I can do for the moment. I suggest you keep them covered for the next couple of days, at least. You don't want them to get infected."

She looked at her hands. "Yeah, right. Like that's going to happen. I've got sixteen dogs and a cat to take care of. Monday, I'm running a water line to add a faucet onto the side of a house then starting a bathroom remodel by gutting it. Sure, I'll wear gloves but keep bandages on my hands."

"You can't hold off on the jobs, even for a few days?"

"Nope. I commit to a date, and I stick to it unless the unforeseen happens and I just can't make it. This isn't enough to stop me. I've worked with worse injuries." Her grin told him she was telling the truth. "Don't worry. I'll do fine. Always do."

"Well, at least keep antibiotic ointment on them. It'll keep them from getting infected and the scabs soft, so you won't tear them open. How about I help you get the puppies home? That way they won't pull you over again."

Her smile and nod delighted him. She was a cute bundle of energy. Pale blonde hair tied in a messy bun on top of her head. Dark brown eyes gleaming in a heart shaped face. She had on a pink t-shirt with overall shorts. Digging into her back pocket, Whitney pulled out a cellphone with a hinged case. She took a business card out.

"Here's my card, in case you ever need any work done. I'm typically booked several weeks out, but you might just earn the unforeseen status to get your job pushed up in the schedule." She gave him a cheeky grin. "Especially, if you help me get rid of some of these puppies. Can I put a for sale, cheap, sign up in your office, Doc?"

They'd moved to the lamppost and begun to untangle the leashes. Keith didn't want to have her handle any of them, but there were just too many jumping puppies for him to deal with on his own. He understood how she'd been injured, totally overwhelmed by the sheer number and mass of the bundles of energy.

"Sit, now," he commanded. Again, his firm tone had most of the squirming animals obeying. He repeated the command, and the rest finally did.

"Man, I wish they obeyed me like they do you," Whitney groused.

"I think having a deep, stern voice helps."

She dropped her chin and in a low gruff voice said, "Sit." Several puppies jumped up and tried to run to her, only stopped because of the leash holding them back. "Oh, man. I'm a failure as a puppy mom."

Keith laughed. "Did you walk here?"

"Yeah, I live over there a couple of blocks." Whitney pointed and took six of the leashes, three in each hand. She held her arms out straight from her sides, keeping the puppies from reaching each other. "Come on. Thanks for all the help, by the way. I'm not sure I'd have ever been able to gather them all back up."

"My sandwich definitely helped with that." Keith laughed.

"I'm sorry for that. Can I make you lunch when we get back to my place? Nothing fancy. Just a sandwich and stuff to replace what you fed my dogs."

"Sure, it'll be payment for my doctor services."

~~~~~

Leading six puppies was a whole lot easier than fourteen, Whitney thought. Taking them all at once had seemed like a good idea. Her hands and knees confirmed it wasn't.

As they approached her house, Whitney saw the heads of two adult Dalmatians above the white vinyl fence she'd installed shortly after the puppies were born. She didn't want them in her house or only in her garage. Fencing in the side and back yards was the answer. Not one she'd wanted, but necessary.

"Get down. You know better than that," Whitney called as they walked up the driveway. The heads dropped from view. At least the mama dogs obeyed.

The puppies were pulling on the leads, getting excited about being home. Whitney shifted three leashes to her left hand with the others. She needed her right to open the gate.

Punching in the code to unlock the gate, she held tight to the leashes, and stepped through. She knew it was impolite to go in front of her guest but the puppies nearly pulled her down again. The sooner she could get them off the leashes the better.

Kneeling down, after Keith closed the gate behind himself, Whitney allowed the puppies to mob her. She reached and removed the leashes, shoving each puppy away as she did so. That was the signal they could go for food and water. She breathed a sigh of relief when the last puppy rushed off.

Standing, she surveyed the fenced in area. There was a small child's wading pool near the house. Its rim was chewed up. She'd rigged a float valve attached to the hose to keep the pool filled with water. Sixteen dogs drank a lot. By the fence was a metal garbage can with puppy kibble in it that she scooped into four large metal dishes. She'd tried plastic ones but the puppies had chewed them to pieces in one day. A bench held two bowls for Betsy and Jewels to eat their food from. So far the puppies couldn't reach that high.

In the corner of the yard she'd spread a blue plastic tarp, and covered it with sand. She was training the puppies to do their business on it. Every day, when she got home from work, Whitney had to rake the sand, gathering the dog poop and scooping it into a metal garbage can placed beside the tarp. The puppies had chewed up the plastic one. That was why the puppy food was in a metal can, too. She'd been fortunate to learn that before they were introduced to puppy food.

Betsy and Jewels came over for some attention. Whitney nearly began to cry. Her shoulders sagged as she petted and talked to them. They needed a walk, too. She felt sorry for them. The puppies demanded so much time and attention when she was home.

She felt sorry for Dora, her cat, too. She was terrified of the puppies. They all wanted to love and play with her, but fourteen bouncing balls of spots just made Dora run and climb the curtains to gain enough height to escape the madness. It had taken Whitney three hours to coax her down the day the puppies shoved past her into the house. She had placed a baby fence across the garage so they couldn't follow her to the door into the house. It seemed that everything she did these days had something to do with the puppies.

Please, Lord, let them be sold soon. I don't know if I can handle them much longer.

Whitney was beginning to ache from her fall. This afternoon, after she grabbed a bite for lunch, if there was anything to actually eat in the house as she hadn't had a chance to go to the store, there was laundry to finish, the house needed to at least be picked up, the lawn mowed, and tomorrow was her Sunday to bring treats for the Sunday school class she attended. Oh, yeah, the sand needed to be raked of the dog poop.

"Hey," Keith said. "You okay? I'll bet you're hurting from the fall you took. You have some Tylenol or Advil? That'll help. Maybe take it easy this afternoon."

"Yeah, I hurt, but I have too much to do to stop." Whitney gathered up the leashes, detangling them as she did so. "I have to take Betsy and Jewels for a walk. They haven't had one in a couple of days. The puppies simply take up too much time."

Keith placed his hand on hers. "Let me do that. You go get some pain meds. What about lunch? I don't think you can easily fix any."

She simply looked up at him.

"Well, the puppies ate mine. I'll take the dogs for a walk then go get something for us to eat. You like Chinese?"

"Yeah, but there's a Mexican place closer. It's real good, too." She handed him two leashes.

After he attached them to the dogs' collars, he looked at her sharply. "You go and take those pain meds. I'll be back in about a half hour with the mutts and then go get us food."

Sass overcame Whitney, and she straightened and saluted.

Keith laughed and pointed toward the door into the garage. "Go. I'm leaving with the dogs. The puppies are fine here."

She surveyed the yard and saw several were

zonked out under the awning she'd erected for them. Others were standing in the pool. One was peeing in it. So much for fresh clean water. Others were digging holes in the yard. A couple were playing with some of the toys scattered around.

Suddenly, taking some pain pills and lying on her sofa with Dora sounded wonderful. Keith opened the door for her and she went through.

"Hey, you trust me with your gate combo? I know I'm a total stranger and all, but you can change it after I leave for the day," Keith said.

"If you're going to help with the dogs, I'll give you all my codes, combos and passwords. If you take them away, I'll give you my bank account numbers."

"Sorry, no can do. I can help some but I have a job that takes me away from home from early until late."

Whitney watched as Keith led Betsy and Jewels through the gate, using his foot to gently keep two puppies from escaping. He started jogging as soon as he reached the street, heading in the direction of the park.

Man, he was cute. Shaggy, wavy, black hair, long around his ears. He was lean and filled his jeans quite nicely. The t-shirt was just tight enough to show off his physique. He wasn't muscle-bound but it was obvious he worked out.

Once he and the dogs were out of sight, Whitney headed into the house. Digging through a kitchen drawer she found a bottle of Tylenol and took a couple.

Dora came in and began meowing. Whitney looked and saw an empty spot in the bottom of the dry cat food dish. Funny, the silly cat wouldn't eat another kibble if the bottom wasn't totally covered. Whitney used her toe to mess with the bits, spreading them in the dish. Dora happily began crunching the kibbles. Silly cat.

After throwing a load of laundry into the washer, Whitney picked up the basket filled with clean, dry 'whites.' They needed to be folded and it was something she could do sitting on the sofa.

She was exhausted. Her knees burned and her back hurt from being jarred when she fell. The bandages on her palms made doing anything difficult.

Settling on the sofa, Whitney began folding. Soon, Dora jumped up wanting to snuggle a bit. Deciding her cat needed her attention more than the laundry needed folding, she stretched out so the gray tabby could lie on her chest.

The purring little body tucked her head under Whitney's chin. It didn't hurt her hands to pet the cat. Soon her movements slowed and both cat and owner were asleep.

Chapter 2

Keith jogged along behind the two female Dalmatians. He was getting tired, but they didn't seem to be. They'd gone through the park and along several streets that bordered it until he'd found the Mexican restaurant Whitney had mentioned.

Not knowing what she liked, he ordered several entrees, way more than they could possibly eat. He figured she could use the leftovers. Hopefully, it would ease the burden of cooking. She'd looked a bit pale to him. He could tell she was stressed over the puppies, and who wouldn't be. Fourteen puppies who would grow into large, very active dogs. Maybe he'd help her try to find homes for them all. He'd built a few websites during his college years. It was pretty easy to do today with the various offerings on the web. There was always Facebook, too, and Craigslist and...

Wow, what a change in attitude was all this for him? Thinking about helping a stranger with a non-medical problem. Keith grinned. That's a plus and he wasn't even trying. Thank you, Spirit.

A couple of months ago Keith had been dissatisfied with who he was. Comparing himself to his friend Mark Jenner, Keith felt he wasn't as good of a person. He'd tried his best to be better but his score card was pretty much in the negative range. Each time he did something good in relation to someone else he gave himself a plus one. When he was selfish and acted accordingly he gave himself a minus.

When Keith realized he wasn't able to ever stay in positive territory he decided to investigate the god Mark believed in. One day in the hospital chapel changed his life.

Nurse Peggy Gadsden came in and they spoke about his problem. She invited him to supper at her house with her and James, her husband. That led to Keith reading the Bible and talking more with both Peggy and James.

Finally, Keith realized that even his wanting God to help him be a better person was selfish. Jesus died on the cross for Keith and all the stupid selfish stuff he did without expecting anything but accepting Him. The realization broke Keith. He sobbed out his guilt and faith.

Rather than trying to be better, he was reading and discovering all he could about God, Jesus and the Holy Spirit. Now, every so often, without even thinking about it, Keith would realize he was doing something for someone else that just didn't fit into his natural character. Like helping Whitney out with the puppies and dogs, and buying her enough food to last her a couple of days. That was so not him.

Well, she was cute and what man didn't want to be the knight in shining armor for a sweet young woman?

Once he'd placed his order for takeout, Keith jogged the dogs back home and placed them in the yard with the puppies. He locked the gate again and went to get his car and picked up the food.

Whitney's house was a bungalow sided in yellow with chocolate shudders. The two-car garage was on the right side of the house. The small porch leading to the front door was nestled back between the garage and, what Keith thought would be, bedrooms.

The puppies mobbed his legs as he went through the gate and to the man door into the garage. Keith had to hold the bags of food high in order to keep them from becoming puppy chow. He must have tired Betsy and Jewels as they were lying sound asleep under the awning. Managing to keep the puppies out of the garage took some doing with his hands occupied but he was successful.

The garage was immaculate. There were shelves that were all labeled filled with tools, bins, totes and building supplies. A bike hung from the ceiling, as did storm window panes stacked on horizontal racks. Brooms, rakes and other long handled tools were clipped to a holder on the wall. He was impressed with the organization. No other garage, in his memory, was as neatly or efficiently arranged as this one. A door led to a screened in porch behind the garage that Whitney had protected with four by eight sheets of plywood screwed to the outside. Screens wouldn't last long with fourteen puppies trying to get through.

Keith knocked on the door into the house and waited for Whitney to come to invite him in. She didn't come. He knocked again, a bit louder. Still no response. Trying the knob, he found it unlocked so he entered.

"Whitney," Keith called. He didn't want to scare her.

A gray tabby cat came through the kitchen he'd ventured into and rubbed against his legs. Then she sniffed his jeans, looked up at him and turned around and stalked off. He must smell like dog.

After setting the food bags on the three-sided island, he trailed after the cat and found Whitney sound asleep on the sofa. There were stacks of folded panties on the coffee table along with several bras. More laundry needed to be folded. Keith debated whether to complete the task, but decided handling her underwear might be past the line of appropriate for having just met her.

Taking a moment to look around, Keith noticed that it was spotless with seemingly nothing out of place. She was definitely fastidious about her things.

The house was built with a great room concept with the island dividing the kitchen from the living area. Next to the island was a dining room with sliding glass doors leading out to the back yard and also onto the screen in porch. There were large windows looking out to the back yard.

He noticed the TV hung on the living room wall with a light oak stained wooden frame mounted around it. That wall was painted dark teal. The others matched the color of the TV frame as did the hardwood floor. A large rug in teals and tans lay under the furniture. The tan leather recliner had a matching chair and ottoman. They were positioned on either end of the coffee table with the dark teal sofa in between.

"Whitney," Keith said softly, gently touching her shoulder. "Whitney."

She jumped and shoved a fist into his belly.

"Ufff!"

"Oh, sorry. Reflex from living with three brothers."

Keith laughed and rubbed his stomach. "I should have known that. I have a brother and we did the same thing." He paused while she sat up and rubbed her face trying to clear away the sleep fog. "I brought food. Do you want to eat now or shall we work on the advertising to sell the puppies first and eat more toward dinner time?"

Whitney grinned. "What's wrong with both? Come on."

She stood and led the way to the kitchen. Whitney went around the island, on into the kitchen, and got out plates and flatware. "Want a soda, juice or water? I have milk, too."

"Water's fine." Keith began opening the containers and explaining all he'd brought. There were meat and also fish tacos, chicken and cheese enchiladas, bean and meat burritos, chili rellenos, and chimichangas.

Whitney looked at all the food and burst out laughing. "You feeding an army or planning on eating here for several days?"

Keith grinned and seated himself on one of the stools behind the island. He'd like to eat here for several days if she was here. "I'll eat here as often as you want me to. Besides, we need sustenance if we are going to post all over online about the puppies being for sale. It's grueling work doing Facebook posting and Wordpress and Craig's listing. Takes energy. Besides, a couple of hours after you eat Mexican food you're hungry again."

"That's Chinese." Whitney spooned a bit of most of the dishes onto her plate.

"Oh, yeah." Keith knew that. He just wanted to get a reaction from her. He succeeded. Filling his own plate, he moved over when she came around to sit on the tall stool beside him.

"You said you're a doctor. What kind?" Whitney forked some burrito into her mouth.

"I did? Oh, yeah, you were going to make lunch for me as payment for my doctor services back at the park. Yet, here I am eating food I bought and brought to your house after tending to your poor neglected dogs."

"Not to mention my injuries. Thank you, again, by the way. I did take the Tylenol and I'm feeling better. I'll make you a real home cooked meal sometime soon. Maybe after we get all the puppies sold and Betsy and Jewels shipped off to my brother. We can do a celebration supper."

"Sounds like a plan." Keith bit into a taco and it crumbled in his hands. Whitney laughed at him. He shot her a mockingly stern look. She laughed some more and took another bite. Keith grinned at her as he ate bits of taco off his hands.

"You never said what kind of a doctor you are. Or do you just play a doctor on TV?"

"I'm a surgeon at Benton Medical Center. I just moved to town recently."

"So I should have opened with, 'Hi doctor, new in

town?'" She made her voice sultry and waggled her eyebrows at him.

Keith nearly choked on his bite. He swallowed and said, "Yes, can I give you a check up?"

"Oh, Doc, can I trust you?" Whitney widened her eyes and looked up at him in all innocence.

"If I break your heart, I can fix it, I'm a doctor."

"But what about my body?"

"You've got a nice body. Trust me, I know, I'm a doctor." Keith swiveled his stool around to face hers.

"If that's really true then show me your stethoscope."

"Oh, so you want to play nurse?"

That comment earned him a smack on the arm.

"I think we're done here, both with the repartee and the food. Did you really want to help advertise the puppies?" Whitney got up and began putting the leftover food away.

"Sure. I did some website work as an undergrad. It's even easier now. I think posting on Facebook, Craigslist, and there's sure to be sites dedicated to dog sales. Might even find some specific for Dalmatians." Keith closed some of the containers and moved them across the breakfast bar so they were nearer to her. "We'll need to have photos of each one. Do you suppose we could set up some sort of background that will set them off?"

He could see Whitney thinking while she placed the containers in the refrigerator. As soon as the kitchen work was done, they went into the garage and soon Keith was impressed with her ingenuity. A folding screen was set up and draped with an old red blanket. She had placed it in the corner of the fenced section of the garage. That would contain the puppy that was being photographed.

They worked out the bugs of how they were going to photograph with the first puppy. It seemed dog treats offered taught the puppy to be still for the required few moments needed to take several photos with a smartphone.

~~~~~

Whitney grabbed the piles of folded panties off the coffee table and stuffed them on top of the unfolded laundry in the basket. How could she have forgotten about them? How embarrassing was that? Here she had a new acquaintance, a man at that, in her living room and there was underwear on her table.

They had just finished photographing the puppies. Keith was getting his laptop from his car. By using both of their computers, they hoped to have the advertisements online by supper time, which would be more Mexican since there was so much left over.

Whitney had watched as Keith coaxed another puppy to sit still. He was quite proficient at it. Much better than her. All they wanted to do when she set them in the photo area was run to her and try to jump into her lap, even when she was standing.

She'd laughed at him when they had finished photographing the puppies.

"Well, that's the last one," Keith had said lowering his phone and giving the puppy a treat. "Let him out, and we'll get started working on the images, getting them ready to post."

Whitney scooped up the puppy. "Are you sure you're a doctor? This one sure looks like a girl to me." She held the puppy up for him to look at the defining parts.

Keith laughed. "Oops, let's just say it was a slip of the tongue. Default to the masculine pronoun without thinking."

"Uh huh." Whitney deadpanned. She let the puppy out and helped Keith put away the background they'd used.

She carried the laundry basket to her bedroom and found Keith setting up his laptop when she came back to the living room. They spent the rest of the afternoon adjusting the images and writing text for the advertisements to post online. Whitney was impressed with his skills in an area so far removed from medicine.

"How do you know all this stuff? Weren't you busy with science classes and labs and all?" Whitney asked.

"I worked for a web design business working my way through school. It was easy work, and I could fit it around my class schedule. Sometimes I miss it. Surgery is a much more intense, pressure-filled job than messing with code. But coding can be pretty tedious. Surgery never is. Each person is different. You never know what you're going to find when you open someone up."

Whitney scrunched up her nose at the expression on Keith's face. She couldn't imagine being excited at the thought of cutting into a person. "Yuck. Don't want to go there. I'll stick to home repairs, thank you very much. But I do understand what you mean. It's pretty typical for a remodel job to grow because of unexpected findings in the walls. Non-code wiring or plumbing. Termites or other critters needing to be removed. Plaster and drywall cover up a lot of nasty things, just like skin does I'm sure."

"Yeah," Keith said, distracted by the task he was focusing on.

Whitney looked at the time on her computer desktop. No wonder her stomach was calling. It was after seven PM. "How about something to eat? I have Mexican and Mexican. Which would you like?"

Keith glanced up and grinned. "I'll take Mexican. Can I help?"

"Nope, you finish up while I get the food. You're quicker and better at this than I am. Give me an electric drill, and I'll out screw you any day of the week." Realizing what she'd just said when his head jerked up to look at her, Whitney felt her face heat with an intense rush. "I'll just head to the kitchen now. Forget my last sentence."

Whitney slunk into the kitchen, not able to believe she'd just said that. Wow, a verse from James came to mind. He who can tame the tongue. Man, did she need to work on that?

Today had been one embarrassing moment after another. First, being pulled over by the puppies who ate Keith's sandwich. Then him having to wake her up when he got back from walking Betsy and Jewels, and buying her enough food for a week. Then the underwear on the table, and now the comment she'd just made. What a way to impress a new guy?

Impressing men wasn't something she was proficient at. Many men were intimidated by what she did for a living. Others simply didn't find her interesting enough for a second or third date. The feeling was usually mutual.

She pushed the thoughts aside and got out the containers of food and a couple of plates. They could dish up what they wanted and nuke it.

"All done. I think we've got the info about the puppies all over the web. Let's pray new owners come out of the woodwork really fast for you." Keith came into the kitchen stretching his arms above his head.

"How can I ever thank you for all the help you've been to me today? I can't believe how much you did and we got accomplished. Thank you."

"Other than you being hurt by your fall, it's been a great day. I've enjoyed doing something entirely different than my normal activities."

Chapter 3

After church on Sunday, Keith went to lunch with Kyria and Mark Jenner. Mark had been a good friend during medical school, and they'd worked at the same hospital until the newly wed Jenners had moved to Benton, Mark accepting the position as the head hospitalist. He'd contacted Keith with news of the surgical opening. It had been shortly after accepting Jesus as his Savior. Keith thought it was an opportunity for a new start on his new life in Christ.

Kyria had suggested they go Mexican, but Keith laughed and offered to buy lunch at local Italian instead. She'd looked at him funny, and he said he'd explain once they were at the restaurant.

"Okay, so what's the deal with Mexican? You like Mexican," Kyria said once they were seated, and looking at their menus.

Keith chuckled. "I had a very unusual day. I even was able to up my goodness score by plus four."

They all laughed at Keith's scorekeeping of his 'good' deeds and thoughts versus his 'bad' ones. The waitress came and took their order and then Kyria and Mark sat looking at Keith. They were apparently waiting for the story behind his comment.

"You're not interested in a Dalmatian puppy, are you? I know where you can get a registered one, or more, cheap. At least for registered Dalmatians."

"I don't think Mini and Cece would appreciate a puppy of any kind," Kyria said. They were her two Minuet cats. They were identical siblings, except Mini had extremely short legs.

Keith went on to tell of his encounter with fourteen spotted puppies and their owner. Their food arrived, and he paused for Mark to say grace, then continued his tale as they ate. As Keith talked, he caught Mark and Kyria exchanging glances. When he stopped, he waited for whatever question or comment they had.

"You seem interested in her in a more than friendly way," Mark finally said.

"I might be. She's smart, funny, trips over her tongue some. I think you'd like her."

"Is she a believer?" This time it was Kyria who spoke.

"Don't know. It didn't come up." Keith took a sip of water.

"As a believer, it's important for you to date and marry a believer."

"It is? Why?" It was the first time Keith had heard of this, but then there were lots he didn't know yet.

"Your faith is important to you, right?" Mark asked after contemplating for a bit.

"Yeah, real important."

"What if the woman you marry doesn't care at all about Christ? Doesn't attend church, read the Bible, pray? Would that make any difference to you?"

"I'm not sure. Why would it?" Keith asked

"What did you focus on before you accepted Jesus as your Savior?"

Keith grinned. "Wine, women and whatever I wanted to buy."

"And how does that fit in with your priorities now?" Kyria asked.

Keith thought for a few moments. "I think I see what you mean. I'd be wanting to deepen my relationship with the Lord, and she'd be trying to fill her life with other stuff."

"Yeah, that space you attempted to fill with everything but God, until you found Him, that is." Mark took a sip of his drink.

"So," Kyria asked. "What's her name?"

"Whitney Houston."

Mark started laughing. "Hey, she died a couple of years ago."

Kyria smacked Mark lightly on the arm. "We know her. She does a Bible study at church with me. I've had her do some repairs at houses I'm doing the decorating for. She'll give you a run for your money." Kyria grinned and waggled her finger at him.

Mark rubbed his arm as if it pained him. "Whitney's lived here in Benton all her life. A friend of my sister's.

The tension that had begun tightening within him eased at her words. Whitney was a believer. Or at least she attended church. He'd learned that just because someone went to church didn't mean they were a believer.

But, it was a relief to know he didn't have to end

what he thought might be a promising relationship because she wasn't a believer. That would have been a bummer. Not that Keith was looking for rings or anything, but Whitney was the first woman he'd met since he'd moved to Benton who had interested him in the least.

~~~~~

Whitney finished texting her brother Evan letting him know she was selling the puppies and keeping the money. She'd be selling Betsy and Jewels, too, if he didn't come for them or send the funds to have them shipped to him.

She'd taken Monday off since her hands and knees were still bothering her. It gave her time to get some things done around the house. She also took some time to just rest. Whitney realized she had been keeping too busy a schedule. With the added work of the puppies, she really needed to begin her day a bit later and end it a little earlier. She didn't need to end up injuring herself more seriously because she was tired.

Part of her morning was spent calling her upcoming clients and explaining that the jobs would be delayed a bit. Only one wasn't okay with the change and canceled. She figured he'd call around trying to find another person who would do the small tile replacement job and call her back. Whitney wasn't sure she would accept it. There was enough work that she didn't need unreasonable clients.

Her phone chimed. She figured it would be Evan chastising her for the threat to ship him the dogs, so she was surprised when it was an inquiry about a puppy. She called the number, barely holding in her excitement.

Ten minutes later she jumped up and down, dancing around her living room. She'd sold, not one, but two puppies. The family had always wanted Dalmatians, and since the price was lower than most breeders, they decided to look into making their dream come true.

Whitney didn't understand the desire for one of the spotted animals, let alone two, but she'd take their money and let them have their choice. It would be another ten days before they would pick up their puppies, but she didn't care. Two of them were going to their forever home. As long as it wasn't her home, she was satisfied.

Whitney looked at the time. Not sure of Keith's schedule, she texted, *'CALL ME PLEASE.'* Yes, she knew it was impolite to use all capitals, but this news was worth it. Soon she'd be down to twelve puppies. If Evan would contact her about the mama dogs, she'd be in heaven.

When her phone rang, vibrating in her hand, Whitney jerked, almost dropping it. She looked at the ID and smiled.

"Hi," she said. "Guess what."

"You sold a puppy."

"Ah, man. You guessed." Whitney knew she shouldn't be disappointed that he'd known her news, but she was. "No, actually, you didn't. I sold two. They are coming a week from Saturday to pick them up. They will choose when they get here. I told them some might be gone by then, but they said it didn't matter. With fourteen to choose from, they could surely find two they wanted. Isn't it great?

"Now, I just want Evan to either come to get the mama dogs or send money to have me ship them. I texted him, but he hasn't replied. Well, it hasn't been very long, but his track record isn't good."

She took a breath to say more when Keith spoke.

"Congratulations on selling two puppies. I'm glad our postings worked. Let's pray the rest sell quickly."

"Oh, you're a believer?" Whitney felt a relief she wasn't expecting.

"Yeah, a new one. Don't know much yet, but it's changed my life. Hey, I gotta go. I have surgery in thirty minutes. Need to get ready. Thanks for letting me know."

Whitney wasn't sure about how she felt. She was delighted he was a believer. That meant a relationship between them might be possible. But he hadn't asked to see her again.

Her phone chirped. It was Keith texting.

"Should be finished by 6. Want to get supper?"

Whitney smiled and texted back. *"Yeah, not Mexican."*

"Had 2 much of that lately?"

"Just a bit. ;)"

"Will text when leaving."

"Ok."

Whitney reveled in the knowledge that Keith wanted to go to dinner with her. They were going out on a date. At least she thought of it as a date. He'd asked her to dinner, was picking her up and presumably going to pay for dinner. That counted as a date. Right?

A date! What was she going to wear? How dressed up was she supposed to be? Should she wear a dress, or jeans or dress pants? How much makeup? Should she put her hair up or leave it down or pull it back? So many critical decisions and so little time to make them. Plus she had to tend to the dogs and shower.

She'd love to have time for a relaxing bath but by the time she got the rest of the chores done and the dogs dealt with she wouldn't have time. Dogs, especially puppies, simply took so much more work than cats.

Once she got everything finished, Whitney flew into the shower and then nearly made herself dizzy by leaning over to dry her hair, so it fluffed more.

She'd decided to wear a blue and green sundress with a yellow bolero jacket since it was casual, but would also be appropriate if Keith took her to a fancier restaurant. Her gladiator sandals gave her confidence since they were so very cute, buckling around her ankles.

Just as she finished her makeup, her cellphone chimed.

"Leaving hospital. 10 min."

She texted back. *"I'm ready."*

His reply was a funny smiley emoji.

Whitney went outside to wait for him. She wanted to spend a bit of time with the puppies, and Betsy and Jewels. As much as she wanted to get rid of them all, they were kind of funny.

Right now the mama dogs were standing on the wooden cover for the hot tub she'd installed last year. They were looking down with expressions of disgust as the puppies jumped, yipped and barked up at them. Ever since they had quit nursing their offspring, Betsy and Jewels had to get away from the pups any way they could. Poor things.

When the puppies saw Whitney, they came tumbling over each other to greet her. Not wanting to get her dress dirty she went back into the garage to get the treat jar. Then she threw several at a time to different parts of the yard. Immediately she was abandoned as the spotted horde headed after the treats.

"Come on, Jewels. Come on, Betsy. Let's hide you away from them for a while."

The dogs jumped down and ran into the garage. Whitney gave each dog several treats and filled a bowl with water and another with kibble. The dogs settled on an old blanket lying on the floor.

"You'll be safe in here while I'm gone. I won't be that long." She patted each dog then went back outside, taking the jar of treats with her. Whitney had thrown another round of treats across the yard when she heard laughter behind her. Turning, she saw Keith coming into the yard.

"I see you didn't change the gate code," he said.

"If you can't trust the doctor you posted puppy for sale ads with who can you trust?"

They were now surrounded. Yips, growls, barks filled the air. They watched for a few minutes, then Whitney said, "I'll throw another round of treats, and we'll make our escape while they go after them."

"Here, let me." Keith took the jar and grabbed a handful of treats. He threw them farther than she could, and the puppies took off running over each other. "Let's go."

Keith grabbed Whitney's hand, and they made a quick exit. Keith set the jar by the gate while

Whitney closed it, making sure it latched.

The Austin Healey Mark 3 was parked in her driveway. "Wow, I get to ride in the Healey. Should I feel privileged?"

"Only if you want to. Before I accepted Christ, I'd have said yes. Actually, I probably wouldn't have brought it for you to ride in. It was my pride and joy. Only very special occasions warranted allowing anyone besides me to be in the car."

"Oh, so I'm not a very special occasion, huh?"

"Ah, um," Keith stammered and stuttered.

Whitney began to laugh. "I understand, but you might want to rethink how you explain that."

"Yeah, right. Let me see. The car doesn't mean as much to me now that I focus more on God than on material things. I'm more interested in the person I'm with than the car I drive. How's that? Better?"

Whitney lifted her nose just a bit and looked down it at him, pressing her lips together. "Somewhat. I'll see how the rest of the evening goes before I render final judgment."

"I may be a new believer, but I seem to remember a verse in Romans saying there's no condemnation in Christ."

"Oh, man. Shot down very well."

They continued along the road in silence for a few minutes. "I was glad to see that our work on Saturday has started to pay off," Keith said.

"Me, too. I was really surprised to get the text. Then when they wanted two puppies. Wow! I was over the moon."

"The first two of many." Keith flipped on his turn signal. It seemed they were doing Italian tonight as they were pulling into Bonacelli's Italian Garden. "I hope you like Italian. If not, we can go somewhere else."

"Do they serve food?"

Keith chuckled. "Yeah."

"Then I like it."

They parked at the far edge of the parking lot, away from all the other cars.

"I thought the car wasn't as important as it used to be." Whitney teased.

"It's not, but I'm not stupid. I know how much it's worth and keeping it in pristine condition helps retain the value."

Whitney's heart did a little flip when he took hold of her hand as they walked to the building. He kept it in his until they reached the table and he let go to hold her chair while she seated herself.

The waiter explained the specials and took their drink orders, then left them to peruse the menus. Soon, he was back placing a glass in front of each of them. They gave him their orders then settled back to wait for their salads.

"You know," Whitney said. "Even though the spotted horde is a lot of work they are cute. Funny, too. It's fun to watch them play with each other. This morning there was a line of them each chasing another puppy's tail. I don't know how it started, but suddenly there were five puppies running in a line each trying to attack the tail in front of him. I laughed so hard."

Keith grinned at her while she chuckled at the memory.

"They've grown so much too. Did you know they

are born all white, no spots? I thought something was wrong with them at first. I called the vet. He laughed at me. No, not really at me. Just laughed. He said they were fine and the spots would come in a few weeks. They did.

"Betsy and Jewels are such good mothers, too. They were born in the garage in a refrigerator box I turned on its side and put old blankets in. I went to the Salvation Army and bought several blankets and towels. Fourteen puppies pee and poop a lot before they are able to be outside and even begin to start training.

"They'd sleep all in a big lump. It's a wonder they didn't smother each other. I saw one of the mamas nosing around the huddle. I think they were making sure none were being squished."

"I'll bet they were cute when they were newborn," Keith said.

"Yeah, though they became less cute when they started to eat the box and get out. That's when I had to put up the baby fence. It's when I fenced in the yard, too. I didn't want to, but it probably increased the value of the house. People like having the fencing already in when they buy a house."

The waiter brought their salads.

"You thinking of selling?" Keith asked.

"No, but I'm always looking to increase the value of my house. Some improvements don't, others do. Fencing the yard does."

"Do you think you might want to keep a puppy? After all, you're their human mommy."

Whitney thought about that while she ate a bite of tomato. "No, I know one dog is a whole lot less work than sixteen, but I did some research on Dalmatians. They are really high energy dogs and need a lot of exercise. I don't think I'll want to come home from work and have to take it for a run, or throw a ball for it to chase. It wouldn't be fair for the dog. I want them to have a happy life. Dalmatians can get destructive if they aren't kept active enough."

"You could have a treadmill for it. I've seen videos of dogs running on treadmills."

Whitney made a face at him. "Do you like running on treadmills?"

"Well, no."

"But you'd sentence a dog to run on one?" She twisted her mouth to the side.

Keith laughed. "No, I wouldn't want to do that."

"See why I don't want to keep one?"

"Yeah, I do."

Just then their entrees came, and for a while, they concentrated on enjoying the food.

"You said you were a new believer," Whitney said between bites. "How long?"

Keith thought for a moment and grinned. "Three months today, as a matter of fact. I'm still a newbie."

"Well, this is a special occasion. Seems riding in the Healey was appropriate." Whitney grinned at him.

He smiled back. "I guess you're right. Shall we have dessert to celebrate?"

"I think that's an excellent idea."

Chapter 4

The following Saturday Whitney waited anxiously for the family who wanted two puppies to arrive. What if they didn't show up? There had been another inquiry about a puppy, but they wanted to think about it some more. Whitney didn't figure they would call back.

Whitney had figured out how much she'd spent on the whole dog thing. Not counting the yard fence, which was a permanent feature for the house, the price she was charging for the puppies would cover the cost of having them. She wouldn't make a lot of money on each one, but she'd make more if they sold quickly. Her time caring for them wasn't included.

Just at the time they'd agreed upon the family pulled into the driveway. Three boys tumbled out of the back of the SUV before the car was barely stopped. The man and woman who emerged were both long and lean. Whitney thought they might be runners. Their legs had that whipcord-like appearance.

"Hello, welcome. I'm Whitney." They introduced

themselves as Rob and Melissa Hawkins. Soon they were all in the backyard surrounded by excited puppies. Betsy and Jewels were running along the fence line working off some energy and staying ahead of the spotted horde.

The boys got down on the ground and puppies began mobbing each one. They lay laughing as the dogs wrestled all over them. They started begging to each have one, pleading as they each held one up saying, "I want this one." When the puppy wriggled out of their hands, the boys would grab another saying the same thing.

Whitney, who'd done research on Dalmatians, explained how energetic the dogs were and that they needed lots of exercise.

"We've done our research too," Rob said. "We've got five acres in the country, so they'll have lots of area to run."

"Plus, we're runners," said Melissa. "We plan to take them with us. The boys ride their bikes on trails on the property. The dogs can run with them."

That eased Whitney's concern that the puppies wouldn't get enough attention or activity to keep them happy. She watched as the boys played with the horde. The sight made her smile. This family was definitely a dog family. Rob and Melissa were standing off to the side talking. Whitney prayed they'd buy the dogs.

Just then her phone chirped. She pulled it out and saw the text from Keith.

"I'm out in front. Can I come in? See you have company."
"Sure. Puppy buyers."

Keith came through the gate a moment later, a big

smile on his face. "Hi." He gave Whitney a quick kiss on the cheek. Since they hadn't kissed yet, it made her give him a quizzical look. The one he returned was definitely cheeky.

"Keith Austin." He extended a hand to Rob who introduced himself and his wife. Then Rob pointed to the boys and said their names.

"We've decided to take three puppies so each boy can have his own," Rob said. The boys began to cheer which caused the puppies to begin barking as they jumped around.

Whitney's mouth stretched into a wide grin. She wanted to do the happy dance at the thought of them buying three puppies rather than two. Instead, she clasped both hands together and willed her feet to stay still just a few minutes longer. She barely contained her squeal of delight. "That's won—" Her voice came out a squeak, and she cleared her throat. "That's wonderful. Which ones would you like? I will warn you, there are a couple who don't really get along all that well."

"Which ones?" One of the boys asked, concerned.

"You each pick one, and I'll let you know if they don't like each other." Whitney gave a wave of her hand and the boys scattered with puppies following along.

Keith followed the boys and got in the fun of helping to finalize the choices. The ones chosen all liked each other. Two of them were littermates, but all three played together and usually slept in the same heap.

The boys, who looked to be between the ages of six and ten, came running to Whitney. The older ones carried their puppies. Keith helped the youngest who'd dropped his squirming bundle.

"What's mine's name?" The middle-sized boy bounded up to Whitney.

She thought fast. She'd never thought to name them. They were just the spotted horde. "I figured whoever gave them their forever home would want to give them their name. So what do you want to name him?" Whitney squatted down and patted the head of the puppy. He had one black ear and one that was spotted.

"He's Hoss." The boy ran over to his mother nearly dropping the puppy on the way.

"Mine's Nelli, 'cause she's a girl," said the oldest boy.

"Pickles," yelled the littlest. "Pickles, 'cause I love pickles."

Everyone laughed.

Rob and Whitney went into the house to settle the payment for the puppies and get the vet papers and AKC forms. It didn't take long, and soon they were back outside. Melissa had gotten a large crate out of the SUV, and they were trying to get the puppies into it.

Rob finally tipped the crate on its end and lowered the puppies in from the top. He and Keith gently rotated it onto its bottom and carried it to the SUV, loading it in the back.

Whitney stood just inside the gate and watched the Hawkins family pull out of the drive. She waved at the boys who were waving both arms as they left.

She turned and went into the house with a smile on her face.

~~~~~

Keith watched the family head down the street. They were heading to the pet store to get puppy food, supplies and toys. He smiled. Three down, eleven puppies and two mama dogs to go. He sent up a quick prayer that more sold quickly.

Going through the gate, he looked in the back yard hunting for Whitney. Not seeing her, Keith went through the garage and entered the house.

After he had passed through the kitchen, he stopped in the doorway to the living room and smiled. Whitney was doing a happy dance around the coffee table, holding a check high above her head.

"Not at all happy about having fewer puppies, are we?" Keith asked, leaning against the doorframe and crossing his arms across his chest.

Whitney stopped, freezing in place. Her face turned red, and she slowly lowered her arms. Then she ran across the room and enveloped him in a hug as she jumped up and down.

"The spotted horde is smaller by three. And even better, they are going to a wonderful family. Those puppies will be loved and happy for a long time."

Keith wrapped his arms around her and held her close. A difficult task as she kept bouncing in her excitement. He started laughing, and soon she joined him.

"I'm so happy. We need to celebrate. I want triple chocolate, caramel pecan ice cream with marshmallow topping and sprinkles and a cherry on top, but you have to eat the cherry because I don't like them."

Whitney wiggled out of his arms and grabbed her

purse from the counter in the kitchen. She put the check in her wallet and turned to look at him. "You coming? I know the best ice cream place. Did you bring the Healey? I deserve to ride in it today. This is the best day in a long time."

Keith followed her out of the house. They went through the front door to avoid the puppies. "You mean meeting me wasn't the best day?" He caught up with her and held her hand.

"I was bleeding and in pain. No, it wasn't the best day. But you did help with posting the ads about the puppies for sale, so the ice cream is my treat. I don't think I'd be three puppies lighter without you." She flashed a brilliant smile at him.

Keith's chest tightened. He was really attracted to Whitney and was hoping their developing rapport led to something more permanent.

This relationship was different from any he'd ever had. Before, sex was the basis for a continuing connection between Keith and any woman. With Whitney, because of both of their commitments to Christ, sex was off the table unless they married.

It was difficult for Keith. He'd had sex regularly. Now he was celibate. Right now, it was quite a challenge. This type of celebration would have been occurring in bed instead of going for ice cream.

Keith helped her into her seat and closed the car door. As he rounded the vehicle, he took deep breaths hoping it would help calm his desires. Pretending to polish a spot on the trunk he gave himself a few extra moments to cool down.

"You okay," Whitney asked when he got in the car.

"Yeah." Keith looked at her and smiled. "So which

way to this ice cream place. Looking forward to that maraschino cherry." He started the car and pulled away from the curb with just a little tire burn.

~~~~~

"I don't believe you can eat all of that," Keith said as they took their sundaes to the picnic table. The early June day was bright and pleasantly warm so they'd opted to sit outside. The family owned ice cream parlor was in an old gas station building with a curved front window, long since abandoned when the convenience store went in on the opposite corner. They'd kept the fifties gas station feel with signs on the walls and a few restored gas pumps with modern soda fountains inside. There was a sign on the wall that said, "You Won't Get Gas Here, Just Great Ice Cream." Customers could look through a window into a part of the old garage bay and see the ice cream being made. The front part of the bay was seating.

"Of course I can. I wouldn't have ordered it if I hadn't. Won't have much for supper. I'll be too full and have eaten way over my calorie quota for the day." Whitney dipped her spoon into the bowl in front of her. Chocolate ice cream loaded with swirls of chocolate syrup and chips covered with caramel sauce, marshmallow, chocolate sprinkles, whipped cream, and a cherry nearly overflowed the sides.

Keith looked down at his turtle sundae, which he loved and usually thought was plenty large, and wondered if he should have ordered at least a medium rather than a small. Whitney's was the Grande.

She smiled at him, opened her mouth and shoved a huge spoonful in. Then she used her spoon to point at the cherry, then at him. She nodded and waved her spoon a bit as she mauled the ice cream around in her mouth. Contented moans echoed from her closed mouth as she savored the bite.

Keith scooped the cherry and ate it. He was having such fun with her. Maybe taking sex off the table led to a deeper way of getting to know someone. Rather than simply looking for the physical pleasure, he was learning more about Whitney than he had any of the women he'd gone out with before.

"I think it's appropriate that we came to Spot's Ice Cream Station. You having all those Dalmatians, although there are three less than before. Did it make you sad to see them go?"

"No, I know they are going to a good home and will have a happy life. Those boys were so excited." Whitney grinned then took another bite. "This place used to be a regular gas station when I was growing up. It was one of the last real service stations to close down. The convenience store coming in across the street was the final nail in the coffin. It was empty for several years then this family bought it, did the remodel and started making ice cream. They got a low-interest loan from the city since this area was considered blighted. It's really turned the neighborhood around."

Keith finished his sundae a long time before Whitney finished hers. She was slowing down in her eating and eyed the bowl between bites.

"Eyes bigger than your stomach?" Keith asked.

Whitney laughed. "Yeah, I suppose so. You want

some? I'm willing to share."

"Sure, I thought you'd never ask." He picked his spoon back up and dipped it in her bowl. The ice cream was melting so it dripped on the table as he moved it to his mouth.

"You are certainly messy for a doctor," she teased. Picking up a napkin she wiped the spot.

"We're trained in med school to leave things for other people to clean up after us. I thought you needed some lessons."

"No way." She tossed the wadded up napkin at him.

They managed to scrape the last of the ice cream from the bowl, then got up and threw their trash in the garbage can. Keith grasped her hand and held it as they walked back to his car. He glanced at her. Whitney was looking down, but with her hair pulled up in a knot on top of her head, he could see her profile. Her cheeks were pink with a blush. He squeezed her hand and smiled as she flashed a bashful look at him.

As he settled her in the car, Keith wondered if he could kiss her when he took her back to her house. This slower pace to dating was new to him. He really wanted to taste her lips.

This was the first time since he purchased the Healey that he regretted its manual transmission. It meant he couldn't hold her hand while they drove. They were silent, and he glanced at her. Whitney was looking out the window. The top was down, and tendrils of hair that had escaped her knot blew in the wind.

When they stopped at a red light, she turned her

head and looked at him. A lump came in his throat. She was beautiful. Lively, funny, conscientious and hardworking. She seemed perfect to him. He knew there had to be flaws in her personality, but so far he hadn't discovered any. But then, they'd only known each other for two weeks.

When they got back to Whitney's house, Keith parked and grabbed her hand before she could open the door and get out.

"Hey, I've got to head to the hospital. I'm on call in the emergency department tonight. Means I have to be there and stay over. I wish I didn't, but I'm low man on the totem poll."

"That's okay. I have a lot to catch up on. I'm still trying to catch up on my work having lost a couple of days to my injuries." Whitney grinned. "I actually took some handsome doctor's advice and took a couple of days off to let my wounds heal. Can you believe it?"

"So, you think I'm handsome?"

"Here I thought you'd been impressed by my taking your advice and your brain stopped at the word handsome. Yes, I do think you are handsome."

"Well, you need a reward for that." Keith pulled her hand toward him, and when she got closer, he let it go and slipped it around her neck. As soon as he could reach, he snatched a quick kiss, then pulled back to look at her. She was smiling softly. He leaned in again and pressed his lips to hers once more. This time the kiss was long and more passionate.

Keith pulled back and took in a long breath. "I need to go. Thanks for the ice cream. Congratulations on having reduced the spotted horde by three."

Whitney nodded and got out of the car. Keith waved as he backed out of the driveway. She waved back.

Well, I got my kiss. Two, really. Hopefully the first of many.

Chapter 5

Keith opened the car door for Whitney. She had a pan in her hand which she set on the floor before getting in. Whitney looked mighty fine to him dressed in a long sleeveless dress with some sort of abstract design on it. She had a white shawl draped over her arms.

He'd driven the Healey, so there wasn't a back seat to put the pan in. They were heading to church and then to the elder Jenners' home for a get-together after worship service. He had asked her to go with him yesterday at the ice cream parlor. He thought it would be a good opportunity for Whitney to get to know the Jenners' better.

"You didn't need to make anything to bring. They told me not to. That there'd be plenty of food." Keith held her arm as she eased into the seat.

The top of the convertible was down so she could answer as he rounded the car. "I already had this made. I told Chloe to let her mom know I was bringing oatmeal cake. I haven't made it in a while so I made it yesterday before the family came to pick up the puppies."

Keith slid into the driver's seat. "You were already going to the Jenners? You know them?"

Whitney grinned. "A little bit. Chloe and I were in the same grade in school. We were sort of best friends growing up. I know that house as well as I knew the house I grew up in."

Keith's shoulders slumped. "Oh yeah, I forgot Mark told me you knew them. Here I thought I was going to introduce you to some really nice people that you might become friends with."

Whitney patted his shoulder. "It's okay. I was going to be at the Jenner's today anyway. I'd rather go with you, though."

Whitney's comment made his disappointment vanish. Moving to a new city had been more of a challenge than Keith had thought. Mark and Kyria Jenner were the only people he'd known. The opportunity to have a fresh start without the reputation of a 'player' was a positive. He didn't have to work so hard to overcome his past. It was like a clean slate for his newfound life of faith to be written on.

The downside was that he'd been rather lonely. Sure, there was a built-in camaraderie with the other doctors and nurses at the hospital, but they were all settled in their lives. It was difficult to make friends who wanted to include him in theirs.

Keith had accepted Mark's invitation to come to his church. He hadn't been told that Pastor Hutch was married to Mark's sister until several weeks after he began attending. Hutch had told him that was done on purpose so Keith would be able to decide if the style of worship at the church was one that appealed to him.

Keith had settled into the welcoming atmosphere of the church and begun going to a new believer's Sunday school class. He was enjoying it and learning a lot. Coming from his totally non-church background, there were many misconceptions he was discovering he had about the Bible and Christianity in general.

His accidental meeting in the park with Whitney had opened up a new friendship for him. He was taking things very slowly, a new concept for him where women were concerned. Getting to know her and finding he liked her personality, humor and work ethic brought a wider appeal than just looking at her body and face to see what he could 'get' from her. Keith just liked being with her. Who knew where it would lead.

They settled into a comfortable silence as he drove to church. That was new for Keith, too. Typically, the woman he was with would fill every possible second with speech. It was refreshing not to have to make conversation or listen to empty chatter all the time.

~~~~~

If Keith had any doubts that Whitney was a friend of the Hutchison couple the baby's squeal of delight as the six-month-old lunged at her, nearly falling out of his father's arms in the process, put them to rest. The child was familiar with Whitney and liked her. Maybe as much as Keith did.

"We thought you'd get here before Chloe and me," Hutch said, standing back so they could enter the house.

"My fault," said Whitney. "I wanted to be sure the spotted horde hadn't knocked the automatic water out of the pool. They did that the other day and the yard was soggy when I got home from work and they'd dug up part and made a muddy mess. I had to block off the area. I pinched my finger as I fixed the fencing. See, I got a blood blister." She held up her left ring finger. Hutch grabbed her hand and gave the finger a noisy kiss, much to Noah's delight.

"Thanks, Hutch. It's all better now. Your ouwie kisses are the best. At least since my mom moved to Florida." She handed Noah back to his father and took the pan Keith had carried in from him and left the men standing in the foyer as she went to the kitchen.

Keith looked at Hutch sideways. "You kiss her ouwies?"

"Only when Chloe is nearby. It's a long-standing thing. Goes back to our days in grade school. Whitney fell off the monkey bars in something like third grade. I was a couple of years older and came over to find her crying and Chloe squatted down next to her. Chloe was almost in tears, too. She looked up at me and told me to kiss the hurt away. I think I fell in love with her at that moment." Hutch chuckled. "Don't get me wrong, we've had our battles. Chloe is pretty strong-minded." He lowered his voice to a whisper. "Sort of like a mule."

"And I suppose you aren't." Keith grinned at the pastor.

"Me? Of course not. I'm a pastor, after all, the epitome of patience and reasonability." Hutch placed his hand on his chest and walked toward the kitchen.

"Come on."

Keith followed. They passed where the Jenner women and Whitney were working to get the meal ready to serve.

"Here, Hutch, Keith, take these out to the table on the patio. If you want to eat you have to work." Mark's mother, Heather, handed Hutch a tray with flatware and Keith a basket with buns as they were grilling hot dogs and hamburgers.

"Yes, ma'am." Keith saluted as he took the basket, making Heather laugh.

"You fit right in, Keith. I'm glad you moved to town. Even more happy that you discovered the grace of Christ." She tapped his cheek, and then shooed him out the door.

Several children were running around the yard. Keith had been introduced to them before. They were Mark's nephews and nieces. The oldest three were boys he knew to be seven, including a set of twins. There were two girls somewhat younger and a toddler boy about three.

Mark, his brothers, father, and grandfather were gathered around the built-in grill with Will, Mark's dad, and older brother, Luke, working the tongs and spatula to turn the meat. Gavin, an orthopedic surgeon at Benton Medical Center, bumped fists with Keith.

Keith set his basket on the table. He figured one of the ladies would move it since he hadn't a clue where it should go. Following Hutch, they wandered over to the other men. They were handed cans of soda and greeted.

Just then the three oldest boys came running over.

"Dad, can we go swimming?" He pointed to the pond just down the gently sloping lawn.

"Not until after lunch, but you can put your suits on now," Luke said after a glance at Gavin who was the father of the twins.

Cheers erupted, and the boys ran into the house. Then a scream came from the kitchen. The men abandoned the grill and ran to the door. Gavin arrived in the house first with Keith and Hutch close on his heels. The rest crowded in behind.

Three boys stood, wide-eyed, with their backs against the wall. The women were clustered around the island sink with Whitney in the center. Her arm was held under running water.

"What happened?" Gavin asked.

Keith only had eyes for Whitney. Tears were coursing down her cheeks.

"I'm sure I'm okay. It's not that bad."

Heather was reaching into an upper cupboard. "Whitney was knocked into by some boys who weren't supposed to cut through the kitchen at a dead run. She was carrying a pan of boiling macaroni to drain in the sink. It splashed onto her arm." She pulled out a box filled with first aid supplies.

"Are any of you hurt?" Gavin asked, looking from the women at the sink to the boys against the wall. All three boys shook their heads.

Mark scooted around the rest of the men and gently urged his sister and sister-in-laws out of the way. Kyria was holding the baby and standing off to one side.

"Let me look," he said. He pulled Whitney's arm out from under the water.

Keith moved closer to the island, wanting to go around and assess the burn himself but refrained. Mark was an extremely competent doctor, as was Gavin.

"You got it into the cold water quickly, didn't you?" Mark asked.

"Yes, I was just about to the sink to dump the macaroni into the colander."

Keith glanced at the sink. A pan overflowing with water and noodles sat cockeyed in the sieve.

"Well, you cooled the area down lessening the severity of the burn. The skin's not broken or blistered. We'll put an icepack on it and then wrap it for protection. You're done helping for today."

Shortly, Whitney's arm was wrapped in a clean towel holding a zip seal bag filled with crushed ice over her forearm. Keith moved close to help her sit down at the kitchen table. He was at a loss as to how to help now, and he didn't like the feeling. They had come together, albeit as friends, but his need to protect and comfort her nearly overwhelmed him. That was a foreign concept for him.

"So, what have you three to say for yourselves? What is the rule and why is it in place?" Luke asked.

Keith's focus was drawn from Whitney and his own thoughts to Luke as he looked down at the three boys still standing against the wall.

They exchanged glances. Finally, one said, "We aren't to go through the kitchen while there's a meal being fixed and we aren't supposed to run in the house."

Luke shifted his focus to another boy. "Why not?"

That boy swallowed. "Because it's dangerous for

us, and the people doing the cooking."

"So, were you thinking of your moms, Gramm, Aunt Chloe and Aunt Kyria and Whitney and how your running might affect them?"

Three heads slowly shook.

"What comes next?" Luke eyed each boy.

The one who hadn't responded finally did. "We need to apologize and we probably don't get to swim, do we?"

"Bingo." Luke swung his finger as if striking a bell. Then he jerked his head in Whitney's direction. The boys left their spot by the wall and walked over to the table where she sat.

"I'm sorry, Whitney. I know better and shouldn't have been running."

"I'm sorry you were hurt. I shouldn't have run through the kitchen."

"I didn't mean to hurt you. I'm sorry."

Keith could tell that each boy truly was sorry for causing Whitney to be injured. These apologies weren't just lip service. They were sincere in their regret.

"I know," Whitney said. "You need to remember that there's a reason why rules are in place."

"Yeah," said one of the boys. "Every choice has a constiquence. This one was a bad choice with a bad one, for you and us."

"You boys go sit in the mud room," Gavin said. You don't need to be underfoot while the rest of the meal is prepared."

~~~~~

Keith was torn between being with Whitney or with the men as they went back to the grill. It was odd being the only man in the kitchen with the women bustling about getting food prepared. Whitney was sitting at the table holding a bag of crushed ice on her left forearm.

"You take Whitney outside, will you Keith? She doesn't need to be in here feeling guilty she can't help," Heather said.

Keith looked at Whitney. "You feeling guilty?" The thought hadn't occurred to him.

She raised her head. "Yeah. I hate being hurt and not able to help serve."

"Well, come on then. Outside with you. Your guilt isn't going to make these ladies feel any better." He placed a hand under her elbow and helped her rise.

Once they were settled in a couple of lounge chairs out of the way of the women bringing food out and the men at the grill Keith said, "That was really amazing how the boys acted as they were in trouble for hurting you."

"Oh," Whitney said.

"Yeah, my brother and I wouldn't have stopped. We'd have beaten it out of there as fast as we could. They were in big trouble, and they knew it, but they stuck around."

"Did running away ever keep you from the consequences of whatever you did?" Hutch had come over with a glass of lemonade for each of them.

"Thanks. No, we always got in big trouble, maybe bigger because we ran and hid." He laughed. "Didn't do any good to hide. They'd come and find us and punish us anyway. I think it was more to delay getting yelled at and grounded."

Whitney and Hutch laughed.

"Luke didn't yell at the boys though," Keith said wondering.

"No, but he got his point across, didn't he?" Hutch pulled up a chair and sat down. He leaned forward with his elbows on his knees, hands loosely clutched.

"Yeah, he did. I was impressed with the boy's apologies. They seemed really sincere." Keith took a drink.

"They were. They understand what they did and that they were in the wrong. They saw the consequence that their actions hurt Whitney, whom they love and respect. They've been raised to acknowledge when they've done wrong and accept the punishment they deserve."

Whitney entered the conversation between the two men. "Then they're forgiven and brought back into the loving relationship of the family. Just like God does for us when we own up to our mistakes and sin and ask forgiveness."

"I get it. You're wanting the boys to grow up being accountable for what they've done," Keith said.

"That's the goal. Too many people today won't take responsibility for their actions. That's not what's taught in the Bible. We are accountable for our actions and words. We're to not only go to God for forgiveness we are to go to the person we wronged. Few do that, even believers. I've preached that I don't know how many times. Seems the Holy Spirit keeps bringing the topic to my attention. Maybe he's trying to tell me something."

Whitney and Keith both laughed, then Hutch joined in.

All the ladies came out of the house carrying the

last of the food to the table. Three little boys followed.

One tow-headed boy ran over to Whitney and climbed up into her lap. He pressed his head against her chest. "I'm really sorry, Whitney. I didn't want to hurt you. I just wanted to get my swimsuit."

"I know. You understand a bit more about why that rule is in place, right?" She wrapped her undamaged arm around him.

"Uh huh."

"I'm glad. I'll be okay in a couple of days. The burn isn't bad."

The boy's head came up. "Will we still be able to come over and play with the puppies next week?"

Keith, Whitney, and Hutch all laughed.

"And the self-interest springs alive and well from the repentant little body," Hutch said.

Chapter 6

Whitney parked her SUV at the end of the block. She wasn't late, but someone had already unhitched the trailer in front of the house they were to remodel today. It was the church's work day for Habitat for Humanity. Normally, they would leave the space directly in front of the house so workers could unload their trucks or SUVs without having to haul their tools and supplies a distance. Seems they'd forgotten to leave it open. The other vehicles lined the street on both sides.

Rather than take her tools now, when she didn't know what part of the house she was working on, or where, she walked up the street looking for Alex Hassett. He was the leader of the team she was on. She wouldn't put it past him to purposely park the trailer there before she arrived. Alex had a bit of an ego problem. At least in her humble opinion, or maybe not so humble.

Whitney grabbed the thought and shoved it away. That's not the way to start the day. She pasted a smile on her face and walked up the group of men, teenage boys, and a few women and girls. Whitney knew those of the female persuasion would mainly be allowed to measure, fetch tools and supplies and furnish bottles of water and snacks. It wasn't like that on the other two teams the church had that did carpentry work on mission trips and in Benton for Habitat. Alex was old school and didn't appreciate women who could do the carpentry, electric and plumbing work like he did.

She wanted off the team but wasn't really brave enough to talk with Pastor Hutch about it. It just seemed whiny and selfish. Surely she could work with Alex and the rest of the men on the team.

"Morning," Whitney said as she joined the group. Most had travel mugs of coffee in their hands.

"You're late. We had to park the trailer, so you'll need to haul your tools and stuff to here from wherever you parked."

Whitney noticed several men give Alex a strange look. "What time were we supposed to be here?" She looked at one of the other men.

"Eight o'clock."

She eyed another man. "What time is it?"

He flipped his arm up so he could see his watch. "Seven-forty-three."

"Yet, I'm still late. Huh?" Whitney turned back to face Alex. "So, what am I working on today?"

"You're gutting and replacing the upstairs bathroom." There was a challenge in Alex's eyes. "The new fixtures are over there." He pointed to the farthest corner of the driveway. "The waterproof drywall is stacked behind the shower surround."

"I see." Whitney did. He'd given her the toughest

job requiring the most strength and placed the supplies at the most distance in an inconvenient configuration. "So, do I have a helper, today?"

"No, you did so well on the last project I figured you could handle this small task. If you need help, all you gotta do is ask." Alex turned and walked away from her.

Several of the men frowned but didn't say anything. They moved to get started on their own jobs.

Whitney gritted her teeth. Alex had an ego that hadn't handled the praise she'd received the last Habitat for Humanity day. The homeowner had loved the custom shelving she had made and installed in a nook in the kitchen. It was an awkwardly shaped space that hadn't been utilized until she'd come up with the shelving. The woman's expressions of delight hadn't gone down well. Especially after Whitney had helped out when Alex messed up a simple window replacement.

Now knowing what tools she'd be needing to demolish the bathroom, Whitney went back to her SUV and got them out. Then she headed into the house to begin the project.

Several hours later the room was down to its studs, and she had replaced the pipes that were bad and finished the rewiring. She was tired but couldn't afford to take a break. They only had so much time to get everything done. Working by herself wasn't unusual. She did it every day, or nearly.

When there were drywall boards and large bathroom or kitchen fixtures to move there were some high school boys she hired to help her. Today she had to go find someone to help carry the heavy pieces up the stairs. Right now it was the waterproof drywall that was behind the other fixtures. Anyone with a brain would have placed them in front since they would be used first.

Whitney came out of the house and saw three teenagers eating donuts supplied by a local bakery. "Hey, guys, can you give me a hand? I'm needing these boards brought up to the bathroom in a short while. I've got to mark and cut for the pipes and electric first."

"Sure, we'll be glad to help. That's what we're here for." One of them said.

Whitney smiled and headed back in to take her measurements.

"Thought you'd be able to handle the bathroom remodel by yourself, Whitney. Didn't think you'd need help." Alex's tone dripped with condescension.

"Everyone needs help now and then." Oh, how she wanted to add, 'even you,' but she held her tongue. It wouldn't do any good and only aggravate matters.

She'd just finished screwing the drywall in place when someone hollered up the stairs. "Lunch is here. Come and get it." A local deli donated sandwiches, chips, and sodas as their contribution.

Whitney stood and stretched hoping to relieve the tightness in her back. There was really too much still needing to be done for her to take the break, but she was starving, and she needed to set up some help getting the cabinets, countertop, and shower upstairs.

After lunch, the boys, again, carried things up the stairs for her. She began with the tile work. It had to be done first. It all had to be laid so the grouting could be done next Saturday when they came back to finish the house.

Whitney was tired. Normally, she paced herself so she wasn't exhausted trying to do jobs quickly. She knew, from hard experience, that working too fast or when she was over tired, mistakes were made, or injuries occurred.

"You going to have this done on time, Whitney?" Alex stuck his head in the doorway.

"Getting there."

"I want everyone out of here by five. I expect all the planned jobs for the day completed."

Whitney pursed her lips and placed another tile on the wall, pressing it into place, then sticking in the spacers.

"Did you hear me, Whitney?"

She turned, and a muscle pulled in her back. "I heard you." She stared at Alex biting back the moan of pain and words she wanted to say.

When he broke the stare down and left, Whitney sat down from her squat and lay down on the floor. It still needed the tiles laid on it. That was what had to get done by five.

Her back spasmed. She rolled over and arched, stretching as much as she could. She didn't have time for her back to give her problems. With no one to help her, it would take every minute she had to finish by five.

It was ten minutes after the appointed time when she made her way slowly down the stairs and out the front door. The tools she carried seemed to weigh a million pounds. She'd brought everything down with her, not sure she'd be able to make it back up for a second load.

"You didn't make it on time, Whitney," Alex said, coming up behind her. He didn't say it loudly. She figured he wouldn't want the other men to hear. It was his personal vendetta against her. "All work was supposed to be done by five. It's ten after. I can't have slackers on my team. You don't need to show up next week. We'll finish up without you."

Whitney looked at Alex and simply turned to head to her SUV. Her back was screaming. She could barely move. All she wanted to do was go home and get into her hot tub. The tears that had been threatening slipped down her cheeks. She had ten puppies and two mama dogs who needed to be tended. Betsy and Jewels needed to be walked, something at the moment she was having a hard time doing. There would be no way she could manage holding onto two leashes.

And her hot tub had a board covering it so the spotted horde couldn't get into it. No way would she be able to remove that cover.

Whitney placed her tools in the back and climbed behind the wheel. She could barely see through the tears as she drove home. Oh, how she wished Evan had replied to any of her texts. She knew he was busy. His job, wife, the kids. But the dogs were his.

Whitney pulled into her driveway and turned off the car. She tried to turn to open the door. Unable to move she leaned on the steering wheel and sobbed. She was stuck in her SUV with twelve dogs needing something from her. She needed help, but that was something she didn't ask for.

Growing up with three older brothers had taught

her not to ask for help. They taunted and teased her mercilessly whenever she couldn't keep up. Words like baby, worthless, failure played through her head. Her brothers had called her those and more, always out of their parents' earshot.

Now she was going to have to call someone or sit here all night. Yeah, and that would help her back.

Whitney reached over for her purse on the other seat. Her cell phone was in there. She got it out and pressed the button for voice activation. "Call Keith," she said.

He picked up after three rings. "Hey, Whit. How goes it?" He was cheerful. Tears threatened again.

"Not so good. Are you on call?"

"No, I'm home. Are you okay?"

"I pulled something in my back and seem," she gave a harsh chuckle. "To be stuck in my car, in my driveway. I've got the mamas' to take for a walk and the spotted horde to tend to." She paused and took a deep breath. "I could use a bit of help if you can spare the time."

"I'm on my way now. Be there in a few minutes. You stay put. Don't try to get out. I mean it, Whitney. Don't move."

She could hear a garage door opening and the car starting.

"I won't. I promise."

"Hold tight, I'll be there in a few." Keith hung up, and Whitney waited leaning her forehead on the steering wheel.

Soon Keith's SUV pulled into the driveway behind her. The car door opened and she turned her head to look at him. Whitney gave a weak smile. "Hey."

"Hey, back at you. Can you move at all?" Keith asked.

"Not sure. Haven't tried. Some bossy man told me not to."

"Why didn't you pull into the garage?"

"I didn't get the man door into the garage latched well last night. The spotted horde got in and knocked a bunch of stuff down. Didn't have time this morning to clean it up. I knew I couldn't get through the mess even if I could get out of the car. So, until I'm able to bend and lift I'm parking in the driveway."

"Give me your keys so I can unlock the front door. No sense moving you until we have a clear shot into the house."

As he was unlocking the house, another car pulled up to the curb. Kyria and Mark Jenner got out and came to Whitney's car.

"Hi, what's up? I'm not really prepared for entertaining," Whitney said.

"Keith called and said you'd hurt your back. Asked if we'd come and help you get into the house and settled and with the spotted horde." Kyria reached into the vehicle and gently rubbed Whitney's arm. "You in much pain?"

"Not if I don't move."

Everyone gave soft chuckles.

Keith was back and gave the keys to Kyria. Then he slipped his arms under Whitney and gently lifted her from the SUV. Mark walked along side as he carried her into the house.

"Where's your bedroom?" Kyria asked.

Whitney, trying so hard not to moan, pointed and they went down the short hallway and into her room.

Keith set her carefully on the bed.

Keith knelt in front of her. "What happened?"

She sat there. Her back screamed in pain. Unable to hold them back, tears streamed down her face.

Suddenly it was all too much. The mess in the garage, parking at the job site, Alex's attitude, the placement of her supplies, not having any help with a major project at the Habitat house, pulling the muscle in her back, and the final straw, being kicked off the work team. It all came tumbling out between sobs.

~~~~~

Keith was stunned. This was supposed to be a Christian group working to help a person in need. Yet, for Whitney, it had turned into a disastrous day.

Yeah, he understood the mess caused by the puppies. That he could easily do something about. But the attitude and how Whitney'd been treated by this guy Alex, that was just wrong.

Keith held in his anger until he and Mark left Kyria to help get Whitney changed from her work clothes into something more comfortable. Mark called for pizza delivery. Whitney had to eat something before she took any ibuprofen. Keith phoned in a prescription for a muscle relaxer. Both he and Mark had examined her to make sure her injury was nothing more than muscle strain. They didn't think so, but if she wasn't better by Monday Keith would order some imaging done.

"I thought these people were supposed to be Christians. How could this Alex treat Whitney that way? Why didn't the others say something? This isn't how we're supposed to treat people." Keith ranted as they worked their way through the garage to get to the yard. The dogs greeted them enthusiastically, bouncing and barking as the men made their way to the food bin.

"Not a very good representation, huh?" Mark said.

"No, it's one reason people don't respect Christians, see them as hypocrites. They say one thing but act like everybody else. What's so great about being a Christian if there's no noticeable difference between them and the rest of humanity except that there's stuff we aren't supposed to do? Big draw there." Sarcasm laced the final words.

"I get what you're saying, and yes, it's a definite problem. But remember, just because someone goes to church regularly and says they're a Christian." Mark lifted his hands and made air quotes. "Doesn't mean they really are committed to Christ. Some people do all the stuff but don't really believe. Not truly down deep in their hearts. They just do because they were raised to. Just going through the motions."

"Why would anyone do that?" Keith picked up the rake and began dragging the poop in the sand into a pile. Twelve dogs made a lot of poop in a day. He'd have to scout the rest of the back yard to see if there were any land mines.

All the dogs needed a walk. That was something Mark and he could do. He would come tomorrow and walk them again. He'd brought his old treadmill when he moved to Benton but hadn't used it. Maybe he'd haul it over and see if the dogs would like to run on it. He could put it under the awning she'd erected for shade. Whitney certainly wouldn't be walking them in the near future and he didn't have time every day.

Mark had made a phone call and was coming toward him now. "Hey, I called Hutch. He's going to come over. Whitney could use some pastoral counsel and I think he should hear what went on today."

"Oh, man. Do you think Whitney is going to want to tell this to Pastor? I'm not sure that's such a good idea."

"Keith, this is exactly why these things happen. No one will hold anyone accountable for unacceptable behavior. The men who were on her team should have stopped Alex from treating her so badly. They should have stood up and defended her and made sure she had the help she needed. If no one says anything, it will just keep happening. Do you want her to go through this sort of thing again?"

"No, I don't." Keith scooped up the poop and dumped it in the garbage can. "I need to take the dogs for a walk. Will you go with me? Can't go until after we have the pizza and Whitney's taken her ibuprofen."

"Sure. Has to be hard to handle twelve dogs at a time."

"Ask Whitney how hard it is. She was trying to walk all fourteen puppies when we met," Keith said. They headed back to the house.

"That had to be difficult. She's not very big."

"Pizza's here." Kyria had come out onto the screened in porch and called to them. "You need to pay the guy."

"Who?" Both men said.

"Either one. I'm not paying." Kyria gave a cheeky grin and went back into the house.

~~~~~

Kyria had helped Whitney to the living room sofa since she didn't want to entertain men in her bedroom. Keith wasn't happy about her not lying on her bed, but the look she gave him kept his mouth shut. When Pastor Hutch showed up the venom of her gaze centered on Mark when she found out he'd call the man.

None of the men were her favorites right then.

"I understand how you feel, Whitney, but I had already heard about it all from several of the men on the team. Although they didn't say anything to him at the time, they didn't like the way he was treating you.

"I want you to know you're welcome to join another team for the next Habitat work day. I'm sure the Jenner team would welcome you with open arms. Chloe will make sure of that."

Mark laughed and nodded. "My sister is a force to be reckoned with. But seriously, you won't have those sort of ego problems with those guys. Dad made sure of that."

"I just don't want to cause any problems." Whitney was heartened by the support of Pastor Hutch and the men, but it made her feel uncomfortable. She had fought hard to gain respect as a handyperson. It didn't sit well that men had to go to bat for her. The quality of her work should stand.

"You're not a problem. The problem is pride which is the true cause of all sin," Hutch said. "We can't change the pride in others, but we can root it out of ourselves. It takes work and the power of the Holy Spirit. I will be speaking with Alex about the way he treated you today. It might be time for a new team leader. You interested?"

Whitney shook her head. "No, I've found that, for as enlightened as men are today about women's equality, they still don't like taking directions from us."

"I suppose you're right."

"Believe me, Hutch. I work in a field dominated by men. I know."

"Now, let's see about your pride, Whitney." Hutch shot her a serious look. "If I understand how serious the injury is, are you going to let me set up some help for you for the next few days. Between you caring for yourself and managing to eat as well as take care of the dogs, I think you're going to need some help. What do you say?"

Whitney felt herself blush. He'd nailed her to the wall pretty well with his talk of pride. Yep, she was proud of taking care of herself. Well, suck it up, buttercup. "I'd be most appreciative of having you secure some help for me until I'm back on my feet and going again. Thank you."

Chapter 7

Whitney was very grateful for the help Hutch had been able to provide for her over the next few days. Though she was better by Monday, someone coming to exercise the spotted horde really took a worry off her shoulders.

She had called her brother Evan's wife and finally gotten to speak with him. The call had left her frustrated and angry. He'd promised to come and get Betsy and Jewels but couldn't give a date when that might happen. Evan had work and the kids' sports schedules to consider. He appreciated all she'd done and glad she'd been able to sell four of the puppies. No, he didn't want to take any of them. They were comfortable with her. Whitney gritted her teeth and kept the angry words from spewing out.

By Wednesday, she'd been able to go back to work for half the day. The teenage boys who had volunteered when Hutch had appealed to the congregation to help walk the puppies and dogs wanted to keep doing it. They were on the cross country track team and, though it was summer, they ran distances every day. They took the puppies on shorter runs, too.

Thursday evening her phone rang.

"Hello?"

"Hello, is this Whitney Houston? I'm Chief Robert Othman of the Benton Fire Department. I understand you have some Dalmatian puppies for sale."

"Yes, this is she, and I do."

When the conversation was over Whitney wanted to do a happy dance but knew her back wouldn't like it. She had to call Keith. The thought stopped her cold.

Since when had he become the first person she called when something went wrong or right? He'd been the one she'd called when she first been contacted about selling the puppies. She'd called him when she couldn't get out of her car. Now, she wanted to let him know that the Fire Department was bringing a fire truck to her house tomorrow to pick out a puppy.

They'd recently lost their Dalmatian and wanted to get one. Along with the fire department, the local television station was coming to film them picking a puppy. They were going to be having a naming contest.

Talk about free publicity for the spotted horde. Surely the TV broadcast would bring in more buyers. Maybe she'd be able to sell the rest in short order.

Whitney looked around the living room. It was a disaster. She'd let everything slide while her back had been giving her problems. Now she had a television crew and several firefighters coming over tomorrow.

What to do first? Call Keith, since she still wanted to tell him her news, or call Chloe Hutchison and ask her to come and help get the house prepared? Chloe had called and insisted she'd never forgive Whitney if she wasn't allowed to help with something. She'd admitted it wasn't very Christian not to be forgiving, but she didn't care in the least. Chloe was going to help with something, anything. Her insistence had made Whitney laugh which hadn't felt that good to her back but had lifted her spirits greatly.

Chloe got the first call. Whitney figured the young mother wouldn't stay on the phone as long as Keith. Or maybe she just wanted the option of the call lasting longer with the handsome man who was occupying so many of her thoughts.

As soon as she hung up from Chloe, Whitney called Keith.

"Guess what?"

"You sold a puppy. Or you hurt yourself again, but you sound happy rather than hurt."

"Yeah, I'm happy. Back's much better. And it's better than selling a puppy." Whitney flopped down on the sofa. The picking up could wait. Talking with Keith was much more fun.

"You sold two puppies, no three."

"Nope, but what's happening tomorrow might get them sold faster."

"So what's happening tomorrow?" Whitney could hear the amusement in his voice.

"I'm going to be on television with the puppies."

"Sweet. Why?"

Whitney explained the call from the fire chief and

that they were coming with the television crew as publicity for the fire department. "I'll be interviewed and will be able to announce that there are more puppies for sale. I'm going to ask for a copy of the news clip and permission to post it on the website and Facebook and YouTube. Free publicity. I'm praying that God will use this to find forever homes for all the puppies."

"That would be wonderful. What time are they coming? I'd love to be there but have a full surgery schedule tomorrow."

"Sometime after noon. If there's a fire call, of course, it would be delayed. The plan is for it to be on the evening news. Oh, I need to call my client for tomorrow and let them know I can't be there and why. You know, since I met you I've missed more work than I have in several years," she teased.

"Not my fault. I wasn't anywhere near when you hurt your back, or when the boys ran into you, and didn't know you when the spotted horde pulled you down."

"No, you just came to my rescue both times. Thank you." Whitney softened her voice as she expressed her gratitude.

"My pleasure. Anytime, Whitney. I'll come to your rescue whenever you need me. All you have to do is call. I'll be there as soon as I can."

~~~~~

Chloe came early in the morning and brought her nearly seven-month-old son with her. Noah had been born on January first as the first baby of the New Year. He wasn't quite crawling yet so they could place him on a blanket on the floor with a few toys and he stayed put.

It didn't take long to clean up the living room and kitchen. Last night, Whitney had picked up the clothing she'd left scattered around the room. She wasn't sure the television crew would even come into the house but there was no way she wasn't going to be prepared.

The cross country boys had come and taken the puppies for a longer than normal run so they'd be tired and the boys had cleared the yard of 'land mines.' Then they ran Betsy and Jewels leaving them calm for the excitement of so many people coming over.

Now Whitney was alone waiting for the call to let her know the firemen and TV crew were on their way. She'd dressed in a blue top and khaki slacks. First, her thought had been white pants but paw prints would show up on those more than on khaki. She'd brushed her hair so that it waved around her shoulders.

Her phone rang. She grabbed it. It was Keith. Whitney couldn't decide if she was disappointed or not. She loved it when he called between surgeries. Even talking to him for those few minutes brightened her day.

Whitney was beginning to wonder if their relationship was developing into something serious. For her, it was, but she didn't know about how serious Keith was. He never did more than give her a good night kiss. Granted those kisses were intense and passion filled. But no words of commitment or the future were ever spoken.

She tried to be rational about it. After all, they'd known each other only two months. Could love happen that fast? She didn't know and was afraid to bring up the subject for fear he'd be scared off.

They only chatted for a couple of minutes. He asked if she was nervous and she'd laughed and said, "Yes, of course. I'm going to be on TV. What do you think?"

He laughed and reassured her. "You'll do just fine. Besides, the camera will be on the puppies not you anyway. The spotted horde is the star of the show."

An incoming call signaled.

"I gotta go. The fire department is calling. Talk to you later." In her nervousness Whitney cut him off before he could say good-bye.

"Hello? Whitney?"

"Yes."

"This is Chief Othman. We'll be over in about fifteen minutes, if that works for you."

"Yes, I'm ready. Nervous but ready."

"No need to be nervous. We'll just chat and talk and the men and I will pick out a puppy. You've still got several, don't you?"

Whitney giggled in her nervousness. "Yes, the spotted horde is still very much intact."

The chief laughed. "Spotted horde, huh? Wait till the guys here that. We'll see you in about fifteen minutes."

Whitney jumped up when the call ended and regretted it for a minute. The muscles of her back protested the sudden movement. She ran to the bathroom so she wouldn't have to go while the firemen and TV crew was there. Checking her makeup one last time she ran a brush through her hair, thankful it was an okay hair day. Not the best she'd ever had, but good enough.

She did a last check of the yard for 'land mines' and determined to thank the cross country boys for running the puppies and mama dogs. They were playful but not over the top in energy.

The sound of a loud engine coming up the street made Whitney head out the gate and onto her driveway. There, a fire engine was pulling up to the curb right in front of her house. Down the street was a van from the local television station. A camera man was filming the approach of the fire truck. Behind that was a pickup with Benton Fire Protection District blazon on the door. Two men got out and two more descended from the engine.

"Ms. Houston?" A middle-aged man with a handlebar mustache held out his hand to her. "I'm Chief Othman. These are Dennis Hultgren, Channing Phillips, and Oscar Lorenze. We appreciate you allowing us to pick out a puppy and film it. We're hoping to raise some money for the department with the naming contest. We're going to have the people pick the names by donating for their favorite one."

"Good idea."

"Where are the puppies?" Whitney recognized the local news anchor, Shannon Donavon.

"They're right back here. I've checked the yard but with 12 dogs there's always a chance of stepping in something." Whitney led the way into the back yard.

The puppies jumped up from lounging in the sun and ran to her. Then they noticed the other men and woman and began running around them sniffing and yapping.

"Let me get a little background from you Ms. Houston," Shannon said. "Then we'll start filming by talking with Chief Othman."

~~~~~

Whitney was so excited. She couldn't wait until Keith got there. They were going to watch the news together. At least in her viewpoint the interview went well and the firemen had chosen a puppy. Each time the number of the horde diminished Whitney felt a weight lift from her shoulders. There were still way too many dogs but the number was slowly going down.

Whitney sent up a quick prayer that the news report would bring more buyers for the puppies. Shannon had promised to email her a link to the edited video for her to post online.

Whitney glanced at the clock on the wall above her stove. Keith had better get here soon or he'd miss the news spot. Just then the doorbell rang. She grinned and ran to answer it.

"Hey." She smiled at him. "I was worried you wouldn't get here in time. Come on in." She stepped back to allow him to come in.

"I brought supper." Keith held up two bags with take-home containers in them. "I brought Mexican. Figured it had been long enough since the last time we ate it."

"Sounds good. Come on. The news is about to start." She took the bags from him and placed them on the counter. "Let me get this out and we can dish up and eat while we watch. Shannon said the clip would be later, probably between the weather and sports."

Soon they were settle next to each other with their feet on the edge of the coffee table and plates on their laps watching the evening news.

"Oh, it's going to be right after this commercial. I wonder what all they included. I hope I didn't do too much complaining about having so many dogs." Whitney bit her lip. She wanted to come across as excited about having one of her puppies being chosen as the mascot of the fire department, not that her most prevalent thought about the puppies was that they were a pain in the...

"This is Shannon Donavon standing in the backyard of Whitney Houston. I know what you're thinking and no, the singer didn't come back to life. This Whitney Houston is the owner of twelve Dalmatians. Her two females had fourteen puppies between them almost five months ago.

"Today the Benton Fire Protection District has come to Ms. Houston's to pick out a new mascot. Chief Othman, why did you decide to get a Dalmatian puppy for the department?"

The scene cut to the fire chief. "We lost our mascot, Daisy, two months ago. She was ten years old, which is a long life for a Dalmatian. Now it's time to get another one."

"How'd you find out about Ms. Houston's puppies?"

"The men began looking online and found information on Facebook. There were a couple who bought three of the puppies and talked about how wonderful they were and how much the family were enjoying having them as part of the family. We thought we'd have to go a distance to get one. We were surprised to find out they were right here in Benton."

While he spoke the shot changed to Whitney throwing treats across the yard and the puppies chasing after them. Then the other firemen were down on the ground with puppies running around and jumping on them.

The scene once again changed. This time Whitney was being asked, "Ms. Houston, does it make you sad to see the puppies go to new homes?"

Keith chuckled as the Whitney on TV's face lit up. "Not at all. It warms my heart to see a new family excited about taking one or two of the puppies to its forever home."

"We're going to have a naming contest for the puppy the men decide on. It will be in two parts. The first will have the public submit names and the firemen will choose the top ten. Then we'll set up donation spot, get it spots." The chief laughed at his own joke. Keith groaned. "At area businesses. The public will vote by donation. The name with the highest total will be the name. Whoever submitted that name will win a gift certificate to Bonacelli's Italian Garden, who has kindly donated the winning prize."

"Submissions of possible names can be sent to the Benton Fire Protection District. You can find the address and more information on the station's website," Shannon said.

The scene changed to the three firemen. One had a puppy in his arms. "We've chosen this little guy.

Now, you need to help us name him."

"And we've had a development between Ms. Houston and Chief Othman." Shannon said and stuck the microphone in Whitney's face again.

"Chief, that little man has a special buddy who I think will miss him terribly when he goes. I'd like to give you this puppy so neither one will be lonesome." Whitney gave the puppy in her arms to Chief Othman.

"So, now the contest will be to name two puppies who are the new mascots of the Benton fire department. This is Shannon Donavon with your six o'clock news."

Keith turned toward Whitney. "You foisted off a puppy on the fire department?"

She laughed. "They'd picked the only puppy who had a special friend. He was whining and jumping up to try to get to the one in the fireman's arms. I couldn't stand to think he'd be left behind. The Chief was agreeable to the second one if he didn't have to pay for him."

"Smart woman. You got rid of two puppies and got a lot of free publicity. Hopefully it will lead to some more of the spotted horde finding new homes."

Just then Whitney's phone range.

"Hello? Yes, this is Whitney Houston. You saw the piece on the news? Yes, there are still puppies available."

Whitney grabbed Keith's hand and shook it in her excitement.

Chapter 8

The next couple of months saw the spotted horde grow slowly smaller. Evan still hadn't come for his dogs, but the cross-country boys still ran all the animals so that burden had been lifted from Whitney's shoulders. With the puppies growing there was no way she would have had the energy and stamina to take them all for walks.

One of the boy's families actually purchased one of the puppies. There had been a number of inquiries after the television spot. A couple wanted puppies for free but weren't interested when Whitney told them the price. By the middle of September there were only three puppies left as well as Betsy and Jewels.

Even with the dogs, the summer had been the best Whitney could think of in a number of years. That she attributed totally to Keith. They had spent many hours together. A goodly proportion were at least partially centered around the spotted horde, but they went to various summer activities in Benton and also spent time just lazing around.

Keith had hired her to do a few small modifications

to his newly purchased house. It was modern and recently built. The thought that she could live there quite easily flitted through Whitney's head. It gave her pause.

Though Keith seemed to want her company and definitely liked kissing her, never had he spoken about the future or anything permanent. Was she just a convenient girl to have around? Wasn't she good enough for him to want to commit to? Was her job something that made him hesitate?

Old insecurities arose. Men liked women who needed them. They wanted to be the one who could fix the problems. That she was more than capable of fixing just about anything had been a turnoff for several boyfriends.

Was Keith like that? He seemed so secure. He was a surgeon, for heaven's sake. How much more confident could a man be? He fixed people and kept them from dying. All she could fix was a toilet. Some comparison.

Whitney was on a roof replacing some shingles. The entire roof didn't need to be done, just a small section. It was another one of those types of jobs men didn't want to do. Not big enough for them to waste their time on.

Bang. Whitney hit the wrong nail with her hammer. It was the one on her thumb which she stuck in her mouth to help ease the pain. She really needed to be thinking about the job, and not about whether Keith was someone she should keep investing time with, hoping their relationship would become more permanent.

The trouble was, she wanted to be with him.

Whitney wanted the commitment. Heck, she might as well admit it to herself. She was in love with him. But did he love her? That was the one million dollar question. And one she couldn't ask him.

~~~~~

"It's been five months, now. How are you liking Benton?" Mark asked. He and Keith were scrubbing for surgery. Mark was one of Keith's favorite assistant doctors. He'd missed him terribly when Mark and Kyria had moved to Benton shortly after they were married. The call with the surgical opening at Benton Medical Center had been welcome on more than one front.

"It's been great. I love my new house and working here is great. I thought Memorial was good, but this hospital is better. There seems to be even more of a commitment to quality care, not that Memorial's was lacking."

"I know what you mean." Mark paused for a moment. "What about Whitney? You seem to be getting along quite well."

Keith smiled. "Yeah, we are. She's a great girl. I like her a lot."

Mark's washing moved from his hands to his forearms. "I've gathered that. You spend a lot of time with her."

"Yeah, we get together a couple of times a week and talk on the phone a lot."

"Um," Mark said. "Is it getting serious?"

Keith paused as he washed his forearms. "What do you mean?"

"Look, it's probably none of my business, but she's a friend of the family and my friend from a long way back. If you're just playing I want you to stop. Whitney's too fine a woman to be just another bead on the string of conquests."

Keith turned and stared at Mark. "If I wasn't half scrubbed it'd be you up against the locker this time instead of me. Whitney is a wonderful woman, and I respect her and would never do anything to mar her reputation or harm her. I'm not sure where our relationship is going, and with all the changes in my life in the past six months, I'm not going to rush anything. I'm still trying to learn all I can about being a faithful follower of Christ. That along with a new job, new town, new house, and a new woman, it's all I can do to keep up half the time.

"I'm taking things slowly with Whitney. Things are going well. I like her a lot. Will this become something more? I don't know. I'm hoping, but the last thing I want is to rush into something serious and end up with both of us broken over a failed relationship."

Mark nodded. "Okay, I get where you're coming from. You're right, you've been dealing with a lot. Just make sure you don't string her along if you decide there's no future. She doesn't deserve that."

"I won't." Keith went back to washing.

"Good thing we're scrubbing, or there'd be danger of a man hug." Mark's tone held humor.

Keith snorted. "Don't think so."

Chapter 9

"You be careful up there, chica," Mrs. Gonzales said, her accent betraying her Mexican roots. "Don't want you to fall."

Whitney looked down from her perch on the twelve-foot step ladder and grinned. "I will. That's why I'm up here instead of you."

It had taken much persuading to get Mrs. Gonzales to hire her to clean the gutters of the old woman's house. She had been in her late seventies when Whitney had finally persuaded her not to climb up and down the ladder herself to do the chore. That had been three years ago. Now, yearly, Whitney simply scheduled a day to do the work.

The last of the leaves had fallen, and Whitney had spoken with Mrs. Gonzales at church Sunday letting her know that Wednesday was when she'd be coming to her house. As always, she'd be served the best tamales ever made, Whitney was positive of that, for lunch. Her mouth watered at the thought.

"Will you be ready for a break in about half an hour? The tamales will be done then," Mrs. Gonzales asked from her position in the middle of the front yard looking up at her.

Whitney smiled and gave an affirmative answer while she scooped another handful of leaves out of the gutter and into the trash bag she'd hung on the side of the ladder. One more clump and she'd climb down and move over a bit. She was always glad to get past this spot. There was no real good way to position the ladder. It was always a bit teetery.

"No, Gus. Come back."

The call came from behind Whitney. She turned a bit to look. Something large and white and black spotted streaked toward her and between the legs of the ladder, knocking into the legs. Whitney grabbed for the gutter, hoping to steady herself, but her wet gloves couldn't get purchase and the ladder twisted from beneath her.

Both in seeming slow motion and faster than she could imagine, Whitney and the ladder fell sideways. She heard Mrs. Gonzales scream, then the sidewalk came up to meet her, fast.

Whitney lay there stunned, with the ladder both beneath and on top of her. Pain was everywhere. Her last thought before darkness overtook her was that she wouldn't get her tamales for lunch.

~~~~~

Keith's phone chirped. He pulled it from his lab coat pocket and frowned. He was dictating his notes from the last surgery he'd just completed. His feet hurt and he wanted to get something to eat and simply decompress a bit. He'd been in surgery since six this morning. All three cases had been difficult, with unforeseen complications.

He had three more scheduled for this afternoon. They were supposed to be uncomplicated cases, but the way the day was going he was going to be prepared for the worst. He really wished Mark was assisting today, but he wasn't. They worked so well together. They always had, but even more so now that they were both on the same page where God was concerned.

Looking at the message on his phone, Keith got up and headed out of his office at a jog. He'd been called to the emergency department. That was never good. To have a surgeon called there meant severe injuries. Keith remembered when he and Mark, as well as several other doctors, had all been called at the same time. It was when Mark and Kyria had met. There'd been a terrorist bombing in the building where Kyria worked. She'd been leaving at the time and gravely injured.

"What's up?" Keith asked a nurse as he entered the department. "I was paged to come down here."

"Yeah, there's a young woman who was brought in a while ago. She asked for you. In here." The nurse led him into the trauma room as Keith's heart clenched.

The team was just finishing cutting away Whitney's clothing. Her torso was covered with a sheet, but Keith could see her left leg was in an air-splint, as was her left arm. Her face was bruised and bleeding from scrapes. An IV was hooked to her right hand. Her eyes were closed.

"Oh, Baby. What happened?" Keith was on her right side near her head, not realizing how he even got there. He stroked her hair gently away from her face.

Whitney opened her eyes. They were glazed with pain. He glanced at the nurse sharply. "Has she had pain meds?"

"Just getting them ordered. Becca went to get them from the med locker."

Keith turned his focus back to Whitney. "You'll get relief from the pain soon. You know how it is in a hospital. Everything takes way too long."

She cracked a little smile.

"What happened?"

"You came." Her voice was a whisper.

"Of course I came, and I'm staying." He took hold of her right hand. "Now, tell me what happened."

"Stupid dog ran under my ladder. Knocked me down."

"One of the puppies?"

"No, on a job. Cleaning gutters." Tears welled in her eyes. "Not going to get my tamale lunch. Poor Mrs. Gonzales. She's so scared. You'll talk with her, right?"

"Yeah, sure." He didn't know who Mrs. Gonzales was, but he'd find out.

"Keith, what are you doing here? I didn't think she had any internal injuries." It was Gavin Jenner, an orthopedic surgeon, and Mark Jenner's brother. He'd come in and was on the other side of the bed. A nurse followed and inserted a needled syringe into the IV. It was the pain medication.

"Whitney asked for me, and they called me down. What's the scoop?"

"Open fracture of the radius and ulna. Open spiral tibia fracture. She's going to take a while so your next cases have been canceled so I can work on her. Not sure if I'll have to pin and or plate either injury."

Gavin leaned over Whitney and looked her in the eye. "Hey, Beautiful, fancy meeting you here. I'll be setting your arm and leg in surgery. You promise to be a good patient or will you be difficult?"

Whitney looked at Keith then back to Gavin. "Can Keith be there?"

Gavin looked at him. "I suppose if you want him to. Not his area, but he can assist."

Keith gave a slight shake of his head. "Whitney and I will talk about it. See you in pre-op."

"Okay. Don't worry, Beautiful. I'll fix you up good as new." Gavin left leaving Keith wondering how to tell her he couldn't assist in her surgery.

His thoughts must have shown on his face because Whitney squeezed his hand. "What's wrong? What aren't they telling me?"

Keith leaned close and stroked her hair softly. "Nothing. Gavin's a great orthopedic surgeon. He'll do a great job. It's just— I can't assist him in your surgery."

Tears welled in her eyes. "Why not?"

"Honey, it's standard policy. We can't operate on those we love."

Whitney's mouth dropped open. "What?"

"I love you, Whitney. I can't be the assisting surgeon. I wouldn't be able to handle it."

She opened her mouth to respond when a man came into the room, shoving the drape back out of the way. "Time to head 'em up and move 'em out. This rodeo is moving to the OR."

Panic shot into Whitney's eyes and her gaze flitted

from Keith to the man and back. "Keith?"

He squeezed her hand. "I can't operate, but I can go with you until they put you under. And, I'll be there when you wake up, and every day, every step along the way until you're back climbing ladders again."

Keith didn't care that the nurse was there and watching. He leaned over and kissed her. "Let's go get you fixed up."

~~~~~

Keith exited the operating room and swept the scrub cap from his head. He'd done as he promised and stayed with Whitney until they'd put her under. Then Gavin had ordered him from the room.

The orthopedist had been surprised when Keith had told him he wouldn't be assisting in the surgery and why. Then he'd smiled and shaken Keith's hand.

"Welcome to the world of wedded bliss. I know you aren't yet, but it won't be too long. She's going to have a couple of months with nothing to do but plan a wedding. Chloe will be thrilled." Gavin slapped him on the back. "Get in there and keep her calm while I scrub up. I think Jose is in there already, as is Mick." Keith knew they were Gavin's usual assistant and the anesthesiologist.

The next few minutes had been spent trying to stay out of the way but right next to Whitney. This wasn't something he was familiar with. He was typically scrubbing while these activities were going on.

"Hey, don't worry. They'll dose you with happy, sleepy juice and you'll wake up, and I'll be right there beside you. Actually, you messed up my surgery schedule for the afternoon. They've canceled all my cases. I'd be pretty worthless as a surgeon anyway." He held up his hand. "See, it's too shaky to hold a scalpel." He made it tremble, exaggerating the movement.

Whitney gave a feeble grin. "Sorry to be so disruptive."

"We'll talk about this later, young lady. No more falling from ladders."

"It was the dog's fault."

"And you're not a dog person." Keith rubbed his index finger along her unmarred cheek. Someone had cleaned away the blood from her other one.

Mick, the anesthesiologist, came over and sat on his stool. "Time for dreamland," he said after checking her vitals.

"Sweetheart, I'm going to leave as soon as you're asleep. I'll be waiting in recovery. Being on staff has its perks. Being able to stay until now and be there when you wake up is one of them."

"You promise?"

"I promise." Keith leaned over and kissed her. Then he nodded to Mick.

Whitney's eyes closed.

"You're out of here, now, Keith." It was Gavin. "Don't worry. I'll be careful and thorough."

"I know. Thanks." Keith didn't know what else to say. Instead, he just took one last look at her. Mick was inserting the airway. Now he knew why they didn't allow doctors to operate on loved ones. The sight made him slightly nauseous. He left the operating room and sat on the bench in the scrub room. He looked up when the door to the hallway opened. Mark Jenner walked in.

"I just heard. You okay?" Mark sat down on the bench beside him.

Keith took a big breath and let it out slowly. "I have a new appreciation for family members watching a loved one be wheeled away."

"Good thing to have. You know Gavin will take special care of her."

They sat in silence for a few minutes.

"I love her. Didn't even realize it until I saw her lying on that bed. I suppose I knew it was coming. I can't get through very many hours without thinking of her. Have to stop myself from texting or calling her multiple times a day."

"Yeah, you got it bad. I had to keep myself from going into Kyria's room while she was in the hospital."

Keith grinned. "From what I heard you visited pretty often."

Mark's face reddened. "Yeah, I did, but not as much as I wanted to." He paused, then said, "I called Hutch. He's with Mrs. Gonzales now. She's very upset, as is the neighbor. Did Whitney tell you it was a Dalmatian that got away from its owner that knocked the ladder over?"

Keith flinched at the news. "No, it didn't come up. She just said it was a dog. Who knows, she may not even remember that."

"Well, they're in surgical waiting when you're ready to see them." Mark got up. "I gotta get back to work. I'm just a text or call away if you need anything. I'm going to let Kyria know, if that's okay with you. Only bending HIPPA a bit."

"Yeah, she'd take my head off if she wasn't told."

Keith stood also. He lightly grasped Mark's arm. "Thanks for coming down here. You're a good friend. I appreciate it."

"That's what friends are for."

"Yeah, to help when your girl gets injured." Keith chuckled a bit. "She is an accident waiting to happen, isn't she? How many times has she hurt herself since we met? I don't want to count."

Mark laughed then. "She always has been, and I've known her a long time." He patted Keith on the shoulder, and they left the scrub room, Mark heading back to the floor and Keith to surgical waiting to comfort Mrs. Gonzales.

Chapter 10

Keith stood looking down at Whitney. She was asleep and in a private room. He'd made sure of that. If her insurance wouldn't pay for it, he would. The last thing he wanted was for some obnoxious family of a patient making noise so that she couldn't rest and recover.

Whitney's left arm and leg were fully bandaged and would be cast when the swelling went down. She'd be confined to a wheelchair for several weeks, if not longer. Keith vowed to help her all he could.

Keith was glad Whitney had signed a release so he could not only get information on her medical status, but also could stay with her in the room. Without it, he'd not be given any information on her condition or be able to stay with her overnight. He didn't plan on leaving at least for tonight.

He'd sleep in the caregiver recliner so if she woke and needed something he would be right there for her.

Keith had gone to surgical waiting and spoken with Mrs. Gonzales and Hutch, assuring the woman that

Whitney would be all right once the surgery was done and she'd recovered. He'd teased her that Whitney was most upset about missing the tamales.

The poor woman had looked so upset that Keith felt compelled to give her a hug. Since he was a loved one of the patient, he could do that. As a doctor that wasn't an option.

At least he hoped he was a loved one. Keith certainly loved Whitney. He'd told her so. She had looked shocked and hadn't replied in kind. Then again, she'd been under a lot of stress at the moment. It wasn't the most romantic way to confess a man's feelings for a woman.

That Keith was a doctor allowed him access to recovery once the surgery was complete. The operation had lasted most of the afternoon. Gavin had come to give a report as soon as he'd finished. Pins had been inserted in her arm, and a plate and pins in her leg. Keith knew that meant a lengthy recovery and extensive physical therapy.

He'd gone to recovery and found her groggy but awake. Whitney slipped in and out of consciousness as the pain meds delivered through her IV began working. There would be a day or two of that before they weaned her off of the narcotic.

Hutch had called the cross-country boys asking that they take care of feeding and cleaning up after the dogs for the next few days until some sort of schedule could be worked out for a rotation. At least Keith didn't have to deal with the spotted horde when he wanted to concentrate on Whitney.

As he stood looking at her, a nurse came in holding a plastic bag. "These are her personal items from the

ED. I'll put them in the cupboard here."

Keith nodded, not really caring about them. All he cared about right now was for Whitney to wake up for a few minutes. He needed to see her beautiful eyes open so he could tell her he loved her once again.

Mark came in and placed a hand on his shoulder. "You doing okay?"

"Yeah, I just want her to wake up."

"She'll be in pain when she does." Mark stepped back dropping his hand.

"I know. She'll need to press the button and then she'll go back to sleep. It's going to be a tough night." Keith wiped his hand down his face.

"You want Kyria or Chloe to come and stay with her?"

"No, I'm going to. Whitney signed a paper saying I could. I will."

"Okay, but if you need anything, you have the numbers."

Keith moved his gaze from Whitney to his friend. "Thank you. I don't understand how people without God can handle this sort of thing. And her life isn't even threatened. How can anyone deal if they don't have the hope of Christ?"

"I don't know. How did you before you believed?" Mark asked.

"I've never had someone close to me be in this sort of situation. My folks and brother are all healthy and doing well. My grandparents on both sides, too." Keith picked up Whitney's limp hand and stroked it gently.

"You want me to call Hutch?"

"No, I'm doing okay, really. I know Whitney's doing well. Her vitals are good." They both glanced at the monitor. Just then the blood pressure cuff began its routine reading. They were silent until it finished. The numbers were quite good. "It's just difficult to see her like this."

"I know," Mark said. "Like I said, call if you need anything. Be sure to get some sleep tonight. You've got surgery tomorrow, and with the cancelations today, they aren't going to put them off."

"I know. I will. Will be a blast from the past. Intern days and all that." Keith grinned at his friend.

Mark chuckled and smacked Keith on the arm. "God bless. See you in the morning."

"Bye."

Keith pulled a straight chair up to the side of the bed. He sat holding Whitney's right hand and thought about how fortunate he was to still have his entire family. He sat up straight. Whitney's family didn't know she'd been injured and gone through extensive surgery. He knew her parents lived in Florida and her brothers were scattered all over the country.

Placing her hand on the bed, Keith stood and went to the cupboard where the nurse had put the bag containing her things. He dug through the bag until he found her cell phone. Hopefully he'd be able to figure out which numbers were for her parents and brothers.

Keith scrolled through the contacts breathing a sigh of relief in finding one titled 'Mom & Dad.' He went to stand by the window and pressed the spot to place the call.

It rang several times before he heard a feminine voice say, "Whitney, so good of you to call. Your father and I are doing well."

"Hello, Mrs. Houston. This is actually Keith Austin. Has Whitney told you about me?"

"What's wrong?" The woman's tone changed from delighted to worried.

Keith swallowed. "Whitney's had an accident. She fell off a ladder and was injured." He paused when the woman gasped and called for Glen. That must be Whitney's father.

"We're both on now," Mrs. Houston said.

"I'm Keith Austin, a doctor at Benton Medical Center, but I'm calling as her boyfriend. Like I said, Whitney fell off a ladder and was injured. She sustained severe breaks of her left arm and left leg. She went through several hours of surgery and is resting comfortably at the moment."

"Can I talk with her?" The emotion in Mrs. Houston's voice was apparent.

"Whitney's not awake. She's on some pretty strong pain medications." He glanced at her, then turned back to look out the window.

A man's voice asked the next question. "This is Whitney's father, Glen Houston, what's the prognosis?"

"She'll make a complete recovery, but it will take quite a while." Keith went on to explain the pins and plates and what the estimated healing and rehabilitation times were. "She'll need extensive physical therapy to get back to her pre-injury condition."

"Glen, I need to go to her." Mrs. Houston said to

her husband.

"We'll make arrangements as soon as we get off the phone."

Keith gave them his phone number explaining that during the day he was often unavailable, but would be sure to keep them apprised of her condition until they arrived. He gave them the gate code and asked to be contacted when they had their travel arrangements made. He'd try to meet them when they reached the hospital.

When that call was finished, Keith found the number for her brother Evan. He dialed and waited for the call to be answered. It rang, then finally went to voicemail. He hit redial. Again it went to voicemail. Keith hit redial again a little bit harder. Finally, someone picked up.

"For heaven's sake, Whitney. Will you quit calling? I'll get the dogs when I'm good and ready to and not a moment sooner."

"I'm assuming this is Evan Houston, Whitney's loving brother who only wants the best for her. Well, this is Dr. Keith Austin, a friend of hers, who thought you might like to know that your sister is alive and will be out of the hospital within the week, most likely, but require lengthy recovery and therapy before she can take adequate care of your pets, which she has been doing for months. I'm going to be placing them at the local dog pound if they haven't been picked up or other arrangements made for their care, and that of the three puppies still unsold, by one week from today. I'm sure, if you care at all for your sister, you'll manage to get the dogs or make said arrangements. I'll text you my contact information so you can let me know when the dogs will be vacating Whitney's premises."

"Wait. What happened to Whitney?"

"So now you're interested in her difficulties. You haven't been too concerned since the spotted horde was born."

"Well, I've been busy."

"So has she, taking care of your dogs and their puppies." Keith's patience was running thin. "Like I said, Whitney will recover. If you want the particulars, I suggest you call your parents. I gave them all the details of her accident and surgical repair."

"Surgery?"

"Good-bye, Mr. Houston. I'll text you my contact information shortly." Keith cut the call and turned around to look at Whitney lying in the bed again.

Her eyes were open, and her expression vacillated between anger and hurt.

"You're going to take the dogs to the pound? I can't believe you would be so cruel. I also can't believe you contacted my parents without my permission." Whitney growled then gasped as the pain of her injuries caught up with her.

Keith was at her side in a moment. He placed the button in her hand that would deliver the narcotic. She looked at him with agonized eyes and pressed. Soon her eyelids drooped. As he stroked her hair, she fell back asleep.

Wondering if he'd truly messed up by contacting the parents and brother, Keith sat down in the straight chair and picked up her hand to hold.

~~~~~

Whitney tried to move. Two things kept her from doing so. The first was pain. The second was restrictions on her body. She understood why her left arm and left leg wouldn't move much. They were swathed in bandages. But what was keeping her right arm from being able to move?

She opened her eyes. The room was dark, or as dark as a hospital room ever got. Light from several machines and indicators, as well as a vitals monitor, gave the room a dim illumination.

Turning her head, she saw what was restricting the movement of her right arm. Keith was sitting in a chair by the bed. His back was bent, and his head was lying on her bed. On her arm actually. He was asleep.

Whitney surveyed the room. Yep, it was a hospital room. She was familiar with them. She'd been in them several times as a child. Injuring herself as she was growing up gave her plenty of experience.

There was a caregiver recliner open and made up for sleeping, but it hadn't been used. Keith must be planning to spend the night there. Why? Then she remembered his declaration of love and the paper she'd signed giving him access to her medical information and permission to stay the night.

It was sweet really. His declaration of love while she was in the emergency room. Then staying with her until she was put to sleep.

Then she remembered waking up and hearing him threaten to send the dogs to the pound. And that he'd called her parents and told them she'd been injured. Great. Now they'd come to Benton and want to help her.

Whitney jerked her hand out from under his head. That woke him up. She frowned at him even though he smiled at her.

"How dare you call my parents? And to threaten to put Betsy and Jewels and the puppies in the pound. That's just cruel. They don't deserve that." Her eyes filled with tears. She couldn't think of how sad the dogs would be if someone abandoned them at the pound. Whitney swiped her hand across her face wiping the tears away.

"I wouldn't really do it. I'm just trying to get your brother to take up his responsibility for his pets. You most certainly won't be able to take care of them for quite a while. And you can't expect the cross-country boys or whoever Hutch gets set up to help with the horde to do so for as long as you're unable. It's going to be a long time until you're even halfway back to normal."

That's when the recognition of the pain she was in hit. Whitney sucked in a breath. She hurt all over. Sure the pain was most severe in her arm and leg, but her entire body simply ached. It felt as if she'd fallen from a roof. Been there. Done that when she was eight and thought she had found pixie dust. It was right after watching Peter Pan, and she wanted to fly to Never Never Land.

Whitney closed her eyes and groaned.

"Here."

She opened her eyes. Keith was standing next to her bed holding a cup with a straw. When he held the straw to her lips, she took a sip. Whitney hadn't realized how thirsty she was.

"Thanks."

"You in much pain? Number between one and ten."

Whitney looked at Keith in the dim light of the room. His face was etched with concern. "Eight."

He tucked the button to the medication pump into her hand. "Press the button. It's been a while since you had any."

"I don't want to." She clenched her teeth against the pain.

"Don't let the pain cycle get started. Do it tonight, and we'll see if you can wean off tomorrow."

"Okay, but only if you leave. I can't have someone as cruel to dogs be near me."

"What?"

"You want to send my dogs to the pound and let them possibly be killed just because Evan won't come and get them." Tears streaked down her face. Whitney swiped them away.

Keith opened his mouth to speak, but she held her hand up with the button in it. She pressed it. The medicine would put her to sleep. The last thing Whitney wanted was to hear him defend himself.

~~~~~

Keith watched as Whitney's eyes drifted closed. He couldn't believe she was mad at him. He was just trying to help her. Of course he wouldn't send the dogs to the pound. All he wanted to do was light a fire under that selfish brother of hers to get him to come and get the dogs.

He sat down. Glancing up at the clock on the wall he saw it was nearly midnight. Keith knew he needed to get some sleep but wasn't sure he'd be able to do so. Had he totally ruined her feelings for him? He'd told her of his love for her, but she hadn't reciprocated. What if she didn't love him? What if his words to her brother negated all her feelings for him?

'He who can tame the tongue.' The verse from the book of James came to mind. Had he let his tongue be untamed in his frustration with her brother?

Keith wiped his hand down his face.

A nurse came in. He watched while she bustled around tending to the machines and straightening the sheets and blankets.

"You look tired, Dr. Austin. We'll take good care of her. Why don't you go home and get some real rest?" The nurse patted his arm.

"I know you will, but I can't leave. I won't be able to be with her tomorrow when she'll really be hurting. I need to be here now."

"I understand. She'll sleep for a few hours now that she's gotten some more of the medication in her. You settle in that chair and try to sleep. Don't worry. We'll be in and out of here all night."

Keith gave a wan smile. He knew the complaints of patients about how often they were disturbed while they were trying to get some sleep.

"I will. Thank you."

The nurse patted him on the arm again. "If there's anything you need just let me know. I'm on until three."

She left, and Keith took Whitney's hand again. He gave it a soft kiss and tucked it under the blanket.

Rather than sit back down in the chair by the bed, Keith climbed onto the caregiver recliner. Not real comfortable but at least he could stretch out. He covered himself with the blanket and lay looking up at the ceiling. He took refuge in the only thing he could do now. Pray. Lifting up Whitney's injuries for healing, his confusion about his words and choices, her anger and their relationship, Keith fell asleep.

Chapter 11

Whitney tried to get more comfortable. Over the course of the rest of the night each time she'd woken Keith had been there. He'd given her water, a lip balm stick to moisten her dry lips. Gently stroked her hand or hair. Each time she'd had sharp words expressing her anger at his presumption of contacting her parents and Evan. Not once had he raised his voice or sharpened his tone.

This last time when she woke up, she was alone. Whitney had nearly cried. Tears had slipped down her cheeks. She wanted him there. She wanted her mom. She hurt but didn't want to go back to sleep.

A soft knock sounded on the door. It opened, and Mark Jenner entered. "Hey, Beautiful. How are you this morning?" He approached the bed, and his slight grin turned into a frown. "Hey, what's with the tears? Are you in pain?"

Whitney tried to answer, but the lump in her throat kept any words from escaping. Clearing her throat, she said, "Just a bit of a pity party."

"So you aren't in pain?" Mark's eyebrow lifted.

"Oh, I'm in pain, but don't want to sleep."

"But that's not why you're crying." He sat down in the chair.

Whitney just wanted it to be Keith sitting there. More tears flowed. "I'm so confused. I hurt both inside and out. I'm so mad at Keith, but I want him here. I'm mad he called my folks, but I want my mom. I'm mad he called Evan and threatened to send the dogs to the pound, but I'm mad at Evan for not coming to get them. I can barely stand the pain, and the medicine takes it away, but it puts me to sleep." Once again she wiped tears from her face. "And I keep crying."

Sympathy filled Mark's face. "Can I give you a bit of advice? Don't stress too much about your emotions. You've got enough to do to just start healing. For today, use that button whenever you're in pain. I know you don't want to, but do it 'cause you love me like a brother."

"At the moment I love you more than my brother, Evan. Not sure about the other two brothers. They didn't leave me with two pregnant Dalmatians."

Mark chuckled. "I love you, too, or Chloe would kill me. She sends her best and will come visit tomorrow. I suggested she wait until then. You'll have a pretty tough day today. It'll be easier if you use that button. Tomorrow we'll see if you can move to oral pain meds."

Though Whitney didn't want to, she agreed to stay ahead of the pain by using the pump. Mark helped her drink some more water. She gave him a weak grin and pressed the button. Her eyelids drooped, and the last thing she saw was Mark smiling at her.

❀ ❀ ❀

~~~~~

Keith finished speaking with the family of the man he'd just performed surgery on. It had gone well, and the prognosis was positive. The family was grateful and effusive in their praise. The kind words left him empty. All he wanted to do was go sit at Whitney's side. Instead, he had about twenty minutes before he needed to be back in the operating room.

Keith was tired both physically, from the short night and from poor sleep, and emotionally as he worried about his relationship with Whitney. He'd prayed several times already today about it but wasn't sure God was hearing. Or what the answer was supposed to be.

Maybe if he apologized for butting in it would help. Keith didn't really think he'd been wrong in anything. Well, maybe threatening to put the dogs in the pound had crossed the line. Calling her parents? No, they had needed to be contacted. He'd looked on her chart. They were listed as the emergency contacts so the hospital would have eventually gotten around to calling them, most likely today. He'd just let them know sooner.

Keith stopped in the staff lounge on the way back to the OR and grabbed a cup of coffee and a donut from a box someone had brought in. He should have protein rather than sugar but that would take a trip down to the cafeteria, and he didn't have time. Just what he needed, caffeine and a sugar high. Made for unsteady hands during surgery. Maybe he'd have his assistant do the major part of this next operation. He was certainly qualified to do it. Would give him good experience.

Keith pressed his back to the door to the scrub room and entered.

"There you are. I was wondering if you were going to blow this next operation off." Mark was standing by the sinks.

Keith sat on the bench in front of the lockers and took another bite of the donut. Powdered sugar drifted down onto his scrub shirt. He'd have to change it. Surgical nurses didn't approve of powdered sugar falling on the sterile field.

"I just came from Whitney's room," Mark said.

Keith turned his head sharply and looked at Mark. "How's she doing?"

"Medically, she's doing well. Her vitals are good. She's not over pressing the meds. If anything, she needs to stay on top of the pain. Emotionally, well, that's another story. Did you really say you'd take the dogs to the pound?"

Keith groaned. "Yeah, I did. I called her brother and told him to come and get them, or I'd take them to the pound. I won't, but maybe it'll get him to come and get them. Whitney doesn't realize just yet, how long and hard her recovery is going to be. There's no way she can take care of one dog, let alone five. Dalmatians are high energy dogs. They take a lot of time and effort. She was wearing herself out dealing with them. I know there are only a few left but she…"

"Hey, you're preaching to the choir here. I get it, but you didn't make any points with her. I'd say you dropped your score by about five."

Keith chuckled grimly, reminded of his good versus

bad action scorecard. He'd not been keeping score for a while. "You're right. Maybe more."

"Keith, I don't think she's so mad as much as she's hurting and confused. She told me so. Whitney's got a bunch of drugs in her and can't think clearly. You know all this. Don't let it get you too far down."

They sat silent for a few minutes next to each other on the bench. Keith reviewing what Mark had said. Mark just trying to be supportive of his friend.

Keith popped the last of the donut in his mouth and swallowed the remainder of the coffee. He stood, pulling off the scrub top after tossing the cup and napkin in the trash. "I need to get washed and into the OR. Pray this goes as smoothly as the last two surgeries. Maybe I can get finished and be there when Whitney's folks get here. They contacted me with their travel info."

"I'm sure they'd appreciate that. It can't be easy to be so far away when your daughter is suffering."

"Yeah." Keith pulled a scrub top over his head and slipped his arms into the sleeves. "Keep an eye on my girl, will you? I'm stuck here for at least three more hours before I have much of a break."

"I will." Mark punched Keith on the arm. "Later."

Keith watched as his best friend headed out of the room. He pulled in a deep lungful of air and let it out slowly. Another prayer was sent up. This one thanking God for giving Keith a man he could trust to care for the woman he loved.

~~~~~

Emily and Glen Houston entered Benton Medical Center going straight to the information desk. As they were getting instructions on how to find Whitney's room a man approached.

"Mr. and Mrs. Houston? I'm Keith Austin."

"Call me Glen." The man stuck out his hand for Keith the shake.

"I'm Emily. How's Whitney doing?" Tears glistened in her eyes.

Keith noticed how much Whitney and her mother resembled each other. Both were lean and small boned. They shared similar colored blonde hair though Emily's was streaked with light gray. Whitney's eyes, however, were all her father's chocolate brown.

"As I told you yesterday, the surgery was very successful. She'll make a complete recovery. Don't get me wrong, she's going to have a long hard road to tread." He went on to explain what was ahead regarding healing and therapy. They walked the halls and took the elevator up to the floor Whitney's room was on. Emily was wiping tears away with a tissue as they went.

Keith led them into a visitor lounge. "I want to tell you a couple of things before you go in to see her. Whitney wasn't happy I called you. In fact, she's pretty mad at me right now. She's also angry I called Evan and," he paused. "I told him I'd take the dogs to the pound if he didn't come and get them. She heard me and wasn't happy about it at all."

Glen laughed. "Sounds like her. She was always determined to stand on her own. Doesn't want help or to be coddled. I think it comes from her three brothers teasing her about being a girl."

"What arrangements have been made to take care

of the animals?" Emily asked. "We, or at least I will be here at the hospital most of the time while she's here."

Keith explained the arrangements Hutch had made. Kyria had gone to the house and tended to Dora, Whitney's cat, that morning. She'd brought an extra key for her parents. Keith gave it to Glen, as well as a sticky note with the gate code on it.

"One more thing. Whitney's face was scratched up and has some scabs on it. There is also some bruising. It will probably get worse over the next few days as the blood rises to the surface. I want you to be prepared. It's upsetting to patients when their loved ones see them for the first time after an accident, and they react intensely to what the victim looks like."

Keith saw Emily swallow and press her fingers to her lips.

"Will— will she be scarred?"

"No, the scratches were superficial. It's more the bruising. It makes her look like she was in a fight. Actually, I haven't seen her since this morning. I've been in surgery since about six-thirty."

Glen's eyes sparkled. "Chicken? Whitney can be pretty fierce when she wants to be."

"Busy. Her accident knocked all my surgeries for yesterday off the schedule. They needed my OR for her operation. Now we're trying to get caught up."

"Well, I want to go see her now," Emily stated.

"Okay." Keith led the way from the lounge.

He knocked on the half closed door and pushed it open. "Whitney?" Her eyes were shut, but she lifted her lids half way. "How are you doing this afternoon?"

"Dumb question. I'm angry, and I hurt."

Keith nearly winced at Whitney's tone. "I know. Maybe I can do something to make you feel better. At least I hope so."

Emily and Glen stepped into the room.

~~~~~

Whitney couldn't stop the tears from coursing down her face. She tried to lift her arms but only her right one moved, and it was on the far side of the room from the door. Emily flew around the bed and into her daughter's embrace. Both of them were crying.

"Oh, Mom. I wanted you here so much."

"I know. I wanted to be here, too. This was as early as we could make it. We'll stay as long as you need us."

"Probably longer than you'll want us." Glen had moved to stand behind his wife. Whitney reached her hand toward him, and he clasped it, giving it a gentle squeeze.

"Dr. Austin gave us an update on your condition. You really did a number on yourself this time," her father said. "Reminds me of when you decided to fly to Never Never Land."

Whitney felt herself blush and glanced to where Keith had been standing. He was gone. Tears clogged her throat. He'd promise he'd be with her every step of the way.

"What's wrong, Honey?" Emily asked.

"Keith, he left. He promised he'd be here for me. Now he's gone."

"He told us you were angry with him. He's concerned you don't want him around anymore."

"I am mad, but I want him here, too. I'm angry and scared and all weepy." Whitney sobbed.

Glen pulled the chair up so Emily could sit next to the bed.

"Whitney, what are you mad about? Be specific," her mother asked.

"He didn't ask if I wanted him to call you. He just did it. He called Evan and threatened to take the dogs to the pound. I may not want the puppies, but I don't want them to go to the pound."

"So you don't want us here?" Whitney heard the hurt in her mother's voice.

"I do. All night and today all I could think of is that I wanted my mom." Whitney squeezed her mother's hand tightly.

"So, by Keith calling us last night we were able to get here today, which is what you wanted right?"

"Yeah, I suppose so." Whitney's voice was small.

"His calling was what made it possible for us to get here as quickly as we did. That was a good thing for him to do then, wasn't it?"

"Yeah."

"No reason to be angry with him about that."

"No."

Glen shifted to get closer, enabling him to stroke his daughter's hair. "I contacted all your brothers. Sam and Charlie both send their best. They each will come for a weekend once you're out of the hospital. Seems they want to bug you at home. Something about it being bad form to torment an inpatient."

Whitney snorted. "Such loving brothers I have."

"Evan's coming on Saturday. He plans to take the dogs back with him. At least Betsy and Jewels. I'm not sure about the puppies."

"Keith's threat worked then," Whitney said. Her feelings were mixed about Keith's call to her brother. She didn't like his method, but it did get results. His success added to her confusion. It didn't sit well that Keith had gotten the results in one phone call that all of Whitney's calls, texts and pleadings hadn't.

"Why did one call from Keith do what all of mine didn't?" Whitney turned sad eyes to her mother.

"I'm not sure. Maybe Keith is an unknown quantity so Evan didn't know if he'd follow through with his threat of the pound. Maybe your brother finally realized you couldn't take care of his dogs anymore. Maybe God is showing you that Keith will do whatever it takes to make sure you are taken care of to the best of his ability."

"But I can take care of myself," Whitney protested.

Emily smiled at her daughter. A wistful little smile. "We all know that, Honey. You don't need to prove it anymore. Ever since you were about three years old, you've been determined to do everything yourself. To prove you were capable. You were the baby of the family, the only girl. We all wanted to coddle you. The boys didn't help when they told you that you couldn't do something. It only made you more determined. It's also why you hurt yourself so much. You tried to do things your body just wasn't ready to handle."

"The flight off the roof would never have worked," her father interjected. All three laughed a bit.

"But I learned that. If there are heavy lifting and carrying I hire help." Whitney knew she was sounding whiny but couldn't seem to stop.

Emily gently rubbed up and down Whitney's arm. "In your work life. What about in the rest of your life? How often have you asked for help in other areas? How often have you said, 'I can't do that' or 'will you help me with this'?"

"Or even, 'how do I do this?'" her father said.

"Keith helped me post the ads for the puppies online."

"Did you ask for his help?" Emily asked.

"No, he offered. It was the very first day we met. I'd taken all of the spotted horde to the park for a walk, and they pulled me down. Keith tended my wounded knees and hands and helped me get the puppies home. He stayed, and we posted they were for sale all over the net."

"The spotted horde?" Glen burst out laughing.

Whitney blushed. "Yeah, that's what I called them as a group. They definitely were a horde, and they were spotted. Seemed to fit."

"So, you've learned to accept help sometimes when it's offered. What's so different about Keith helping now?"

Whitney thought about it for a few moments. "I'm scared. Yesterday, he told me that he loved me. That's why he couldn't assist with my surgery. He was with me until they put me to sleep. Then he was right beside me when I woke up. It made me feel so protected, so loved."

"What's wrong with that?" Emily asked softly.

"Nothing, it was comforting. Then later, I woke up in pain and Keith was speaking so firmly with Evan, telling him to come get the dogs. And he'd called you. I felt like he was taking over my life. That, because he loved me, he had the right to just do everything without consulting me about anything."

"Whitney, sometimes others have to make choices for us when we can't make the decisions for ourselves at the moment. That's what we trust our loved ones to do. To make the right decisions for us when we can't.

"Your dad does that for me, and I do it for him. It's not very often. Maybe a half dozen times in our entire marriage. It's comforting to know I have someone to rely on who only wants the best for me, especially when I can't do it for myself." Emily looked at Glen, and Whitney could see the love and trust in both their expressions.

Whitney's eyes filled with tears again. She'd cried more in the last twenty-four hours than ever before in her life. "Do you think I chased him away for good, Mom?" Fear that she had made more tears flow.

Emily squeezed her hand. "If so, then he's not the one for you. But I think Keith's just giving us private time. He knows we would want to talk. Simple politeness would have him leave us alone."

"You want me to go find him?" Glen asked.

"You don't have to, Dad."

"I know, but you want me to."

Whitney took the tissues her mother handed to her and wiped her face. "Yeah, I do."

Chapter 12

Keith paced in his office. He prayed Whitney's parents could smooth over the mistakes he'd made. He'd only wanted to help. Most of the time patients want their parents or children with them. All he'd wanted to do was the best he could think of that would help her and make her feel better. Seems he'd messed up on both counts.

A cell phone in his lab coat pocket rang. It was an unfamiliar ringtone. Something girly, and not at all what he'd programmed into his phone. Pulling the phone out, Keith saw it wasn't his phone but Whitney's. Oh man, after he'd used it the night before he'd just shoved it into his pocket and forgotten about it.

"Hello?" Keith answered.

"Hello, is this the person with the Dalmatian puppies?"

"Um, yes, it is."

"Great, do you have any left. I know it's been a while since you placed the ad so you may have sold them all."

Keith and the caller talked for a few minutes then he hung up. Now he really needed to speak with Whitney. Did he dare go to her room? Or was she still too angry to even want to talk with him?

There was a knock at his open door. Keith looked up. It was Glen Houston.

"Dr. Austin."

"Call me Keith," he interrupted.

Glen smiled. "Keith, I think Emily has calmed Whitney down and helped her see you weren't trying to take over her life. She wants to see you now."

"I never wanted to take over anything. I just wanted to help. I never dreamed she'd get mad that I called you. Okay, maybe I stepped over into controlling when I called Evan, but his attitude really made me angry. Whitney's been overwhelmed with the puppies, and he hasn't done anything. Not even come and gotten his dogs."

"Well, I have good news then. We spoke with Evan, and he's coming this weekend to get at least Betsy and Jewels." Glen fell into step with Keith as they headed toward the elevator.

"I may have good news, too, on the puppy front."

~~~~~

Emily had called the nurse who helped Whitney wash her face, comb her hair and brush her teeth. The last thing Whitney wanted was dragon breath when she saw Keith again. The nurse also changed Whitney's hospital gown.

Although she was still hooked up to the pain pump, they had given Whitney an oral medication, and it seemed to be working. It didn't knock her out or make her thinking as muddled. Maybe that had contributed to her anger at Keith last night. Whitney wasn't sure. All she cared about right now was seeing him and finding out if he still loved her and wanted to continue in their relationship.

Whitney realized that he'd said he loved her, but she hadn't said it back. Granted, it was before her operation yesterday that Keith had told her, and she was more focused on the necessity of her having surgery. Now she just wanted to have him with her so she could tell him.

"Look who I found lurking in his office." Whitney's father entered with Keith following behind in a somewhat timid manner.

Whitney smiled with relief that he hadn't refused to come.

"Come on, Mother. Let's let these two have a bit of time to themselves. We'll go get something to eat in the cafeteria before it closes." Glen held out his hand to Emily, who clasped it. They left, closing the door behind them.

"Hey," Keith said. "I'm sorry I made you mad by calling your parents and Evan."

Her eyes welling with tears again, Whitney reached out her hand to him. Keith came around to the right side of the bed and took her hand.

"I'm sorry I got so mad at you. I should have realized you were just trying to help." She brought his hand to her cheek and rubbed it back and forth. "It's always been hard to let someone help me."

"I've always wanted to fix things for people. Well, not like you do, but you get the idea." Keith sat on the side of the bed. "Whitney, what I said yesterday still holds. I love you. I want you in my life always. I understand or will try to if you say you can't or don't want me to continue seeing you. I get that I messed up big time last night."

Whitney pressed her fingers against his lips. "No, you didn't mess up big time. I did, or maybe we both did. It's okay now. We've both apologized and been forgiven. At least I hope you forgave me."

"Of course."

"Then I only have one thing more I want to say to you. I love you, too. I should have said it yesterday." When Keith's eyes went from dull and sad to bright and joyous, she knew he didn't care that her confession of love was a day late.

Leaning over her, Keith placed his hands on Whitney's cheeks. His hazel eyes told of his feelings. They held joy, caring, commitment, protection, and, most of all, love.

When his lips met hers, Whitney sighed and wished she could put both her arms around him and hold him close. Doing the next best thing, she wrapped her right arm around his neck and held on as if she were sinking. Maybe she was. Sinking into the security of his love.

"Be careful," Keith whispered, his lips still pressed against hers. "You're injured. I don't want to slip and fall and damage you more."

Whitney loosened her hold but didn't release him. Keith didn't seem to mind as their kiss got more passionate. When his tongue tickled her lips, she opened them and reveled in the taste of his mouth.

Finally, Keith pulled back. "I love you. I want to be with you always. I know this isn't the most romantic setting, and I don't have a ring, but will you marry me? I can't stand waiting until you're all healed for you to promise you'll be my wife."

Just as she had so many times over the past twenty-four hours, Whitney felt her eyes well up with tears. As they slipped over the rim and down her cheeks, she said, "Yes, I can't wait to become your wife. I wish it could be tomorrow, but I don't think I'm quite up to it at the moment."

Keith kissed her again. And again. Then he pulled away, much to Whitney's disappointment. "I forgot." He pulled her cell phone out of his pocket. "This got stuffed in my lab coat, and I forgot all about it. I, or you, got a call. I took it, and it was a man who has a pet store. He's had some inquiries about Dalmatian puppies. He was wondering if he could buy yours at a discount so he could sell them in his store. I told him I'd check with you and find out. What do you say?"

"He wants all three?" Whitney was incredulous at the prospect. Evan was coming this weekend to get Betsy and Jewels. There was a man who wanted all three of the remaining puppies. "Heck yeah, I'll sell them at a discount. When does he want them?"

"He said he could come and pick them up as soon as you gave the go ahead. He's about two hours away so he may come as early as tomorrow. I have a full schedule, but I'm sure Kyria would meet him if you asked her."

"I wish I could be there to see the last of them go, but you make the calls and handle the details. Having the last of the spotted horde go to new homes is just fine with me." Whitney grabbed Keith's lab coat lapel and pulled him down for another kiss.

Epilogue

Whitney was horrified. She looked from the hand mirror to her mother, then Keith, then back at her reflection.

"See why we didn't want to give you a mirror?" Emily said.

"They'll fade with time. Maybe a couple of weeks and they'll all be gone."

Whitney looked at Keith who'd said the words. He really thought he was helping. A couple of weeks. She had a stinking Fu Man Chu mustache from her fall from the ladder. Granted it was a bruise and would fade, but still. Evan was coming today and would tease her to no end.

There was nothing Whitney could do to cover the thing. Well, she supposed stage makeup would do the trick, but she was a little short on that. She had to think of something to stop him from taking photos and posting them all over Facebook.

Ah ha, that's it, she thought. An evil grin grew under the mustache in the mirror.

"You want me to warn Evan not to tease you about

it?" Leave it to her dad to protect her. Keith was pretty good at it, but her dad had more experience.

"No, I got this. When's Evan supposed to be here?" Whitney asked.

"Anytime. He texted the last time he stopped for gas." Emily said.

It was Saturday. Evan had left home last night and driven several hours before he stopped to get some sleep. It was now shortly after one o'clock in the afternoon.

The man who bought the last three puppies had come that morning and picked them up. Keith had been at the house along with Glen for the transaction. Whitney's parents were staying in her guest room. Keith had taken photos of the puppies as they were being loaded into crates for the ride back to the pet shop.

Whitney was surprised when she'd teared up at the thought of being without the spotted horde when she went home. Keith had sent the photos to her phone, and she decided to sort through all that she had taken and make a memory book of them. That was good enough for her to remember them by.

Keith, wearing his lab coat even though he wasn't on duty, came over and sat on the edge of the bed. Whitney was sitting up in a recliner. Therapy had her standing on her one good leg for a while this morning. That was when Whitney had truly realized how limited she was going to be for a long while. At least six to eight weeks before she was going to be allowed to even try to put any weight on the left leg. It made her even more grateful her parents were going to be staying until she was literally back on her feet.

"Even with your mustache, you are beautiful. Funny looking, but beautiful."

Whitney smacked him on the arm with the back of her hand.

They'd told her parents about their engagement. Glen and Emily were delighted. They'd called Keith's parents who were happy for him, but a bit confused as to why they hadn't heard about her before. Whitney looked at him while he stammered something about being busy and not had a chance to call. Once the call was ended, all she'd said was, "We'll just chat about your communication skills with your parents at a later date."

A knock sounded on the door, and everyone looked. Evan stuck his head in. "Is it safe, or is Whitney going to throw things at me?"

"I just might, but I'm happy enough today to give you a pass," Whitney said.

Evan came in and hugged his mother then came around the bed heading to where his sister sat. "Whoa, girl. I gotta get a photo of that mustache."

"You do, and you're dead to me. Also, remember, I have photos of you in a Little Mermaid costume, and I'm not afraid to post them online."

Evan put his phone back into his pocket. "Okay, you win, no photos. But I gotta be able to tell Charlie and Sam."

"They already know," Whitney said. "Offensive move to stop you."

"Rats, Whit, you gotta give me something."

Whitney cleared her throat. "I'm not giving you the bill for what the puppies and dogs cost me over the last six months. Consider yourself lucky I still call you my brother."

"Yeah, well, sorry." Evan had the grace to try to look repentant.

"No, you're not, so don't try and fool me."

"That's enough." Glen's tone brought echoes of their youth to the forefront.

Evan leaned over and gave his sister a hug.

Keith stood up and held out his hand. "I'm Keith Austin, newly engaged to your sister."

"Wow, I didn't even know she had a boyfriend. Congratulations, I think." Whitney punched him hard on the leg.

Evan stayed, and they all chatted for several hours. Then Evan, Glen, and Emily left to get something to eat, and then load up Betsy and Jewels. Evan needed to get on the road to travel part way home so he could get there in good time tomorrow.

Whitney, tired and in pain from sitting up so long, was relieved when she was settled back in the bed. Keith sat down next to her.

"Well, that's the last of the dogs. Your home will be your own when you get out of here."

"Yeah, right now I can't tell if I'm relieved or sad. For all the problems and difficulties I went through with them, I do have fond memories of the spotted horde, too. They were so funny sometimes." Whitney smiled at him.

"Well, I thought you might. Just to be sure you aren't too sad and missing them too much, I got you something." Keith pulled a small wrapped package out of his lab coat pocket. "Here."

Whitney took it. It was squishy. Pulling the paper

off revealed a floppy Dalmatian stuffed animal. "Oh, how cute, thank you."

"And you never have to look for land mines in the yard." Keith was leaning close. "And Dora won't have to climb the curtains to get away." His lips moved nearer to hers. "And you don't have to walk him." Their lips met for a long time. "But I'll always be there to tend to every accident he causes."

A note from Sophie

I hope you enjoyed **Spots Before Marriage**. The best thank you that you can give an author is a review. If you take just a few minutes you could help someone else find their next favorite book.

You can post a review right from your Kindle or Kindle app. Just scroll past the end of the book. The form will pop up. Although Amazon says they require 20 words they will post it with fewer.

Would you like a free book?

Seeing the Life

$2.99 value. Free when you sign up for my newsletter.

See the life that changed the course of human history through the eyes of Dassa and Micah.

Dassa and Micah begin their life together in Bethlehem with joy and tragedy. The hand of God moves them to Jerusalem where Micah is a scribe to the metal merchant Joseph the Arimethean. In the heart of Israel they live the events occurring during the occupation by the Roman Empire. Including the stirrings of a young rabbi from Nazareth.

Micah, Joseph and their families follow the ministries of John the Baptist and Yeshua, a poor carpenter from Nazareth. Is he the Messiah who will lead Israel against the Roman army? Is he a fraud, a cohort of Satan? Or is he something else? The crowds cheer him, then want to stone him. They hail his arrival then, cry for his execution. The newsletter only comes to you when there is actual real, news about my books. You need not worry that your information will ever be released to anyone in any way for anything. I hate spam as much as you do.

http://dl.bookfunnel.com/gpoyblit18

If you don't want the book but would still like to be notified of upcoming releases please sign up for my newsletter. It only comes to you when there is actual real, news about my books or special offers.

Here's the link for you to sign up. http://www.sophie-dawson.-com/subscription.html

As a treat, keep going and you'll find the first chapter in the next book in the Love's Infestation Series, the first chapter of **Mice and Marriage**. It's a holiday story that will be available fall of 2017.

Thank you.

Sophie

Books By Sophie Dawson

Cottonwood Series

Healing Love

Lord's Love

Giving Love

Redeeming Love (With George McVey)

Stones Creek Series

Leah's Peace

Chasing Norie

Chloe's Choice (Short Story)

Chloe's Sanctuary

Love's Infestation

Mold and Marriage

Single Books

Seeing The Life

Rescued By Love

If you enjoyed this book and would like to find other great Christian Indie Authors reads, follow the link below. Christian Books in Multiple Genres, Join Christian Indie Author ~ Readers Group on Facebook. Opportunities for free books and giveaways.

https://www.facebook.com/groups/291215317668431/

Mice and Marriage
Chapter 1

The scream coming from the pole barn as Turner snapped the bike lock closed made him jump to his feet and run to the wide open garage door. He grabbed the auto-release knife handle from the sleeve of his black leather jacket but didn't depress the trigger. Pausing, he peeked around the edge of the door to survey the large open area before he entered. Then he slipped the knife back into its pocket and pressed the Velcro closed. He wouldn't need it.

Walking in, he sauntered over the picnic table the young woman was standing on. The thin plastic tablecloth was bunched around her feet as she turned around several times as he approached. Dressed in blue jeans, red wool pea coat, and white knit hat, she looked to be in her late twenties. She was pretty but not stunning. She reminded him a bit of someone, but he couldn't think who.

"Looking for something?" Turner asked as he neared the table.

Her eyes, big and round, spied him and became wider. She was surprised to see him. "A mouse. There was this huge mouse." She spread her arms wide apart.

Turner, who had seen mice and rats all over the world hadn't ever seen one that large, so he merely grinned. "Afraid of mice?" He stuck his hands in his jacket pockets. The early November day was chilly, and the open door made the room the same temperature as the outside. It wasn't an issue while he was riding but tucking his hands away felt good.

"Have you ever had one crawl up the inside of your pant leg? It's a horrible feeling," she said.

Turner was familiar with the experience and not anxious to repeat it, but in a large pole barn, in an urban area that wasn't likely. Being the gentleman that he was, he figured it was up to him to aid the lady in distress.

He was standing next to the picnic table now looking up at her. From his jacket pocket, Turner pulled the velcro straps he wore at his ankles controlling his pant legs as he biked if he wasn't dressed in riding clothes. Today he had on jeans. He'd removed them and put them in his pocket just before he locked his bike.

"These will keep the mice from crawling up your pant legs, though I'm not sure one that large could get up them anyway." Turner wrapped each pant leg with a strap around her ankle. Slim ankle. Shapely leg too, he noticed, then he helped her down to the concrete floor. "I think you might not want to use this tablecloth." He picked it up and shook out the wadded mess her feet had made of it. There were wrinkles and tears over most of it.

"Um, no, I suppose not." She bit her lip, then began to laugh. "You must think I'm pretty ridiculous. My scream probably gave the mouse a heart attack."

"Very likely. He's probably in the next county by now running from you, scared for his life." Turner smiled and held out his hand. "Turner Metcalf at your service."

"Oh, I'm Noelle Copeland." She held out her gloved hand, and he took it, holding it a bit longer than necessary as he shook it. "Metcalf? Are you... Yes, you're Kyria Jenner's brother. I remember you know from the wedding."

"That's right. I was there. I don't remember you though, and I'm sure I would if we'd met."

A sadly shadowed expression crossed her face. "I kept a pretty low profile that day. Going through a rough patch in my life." The smile she gave was forced, he could tell. "Better times now."

Turner wondered what the rough patch was but didn't ask. Two reasons crossed his mind. First, it was none of his business, and second, he wanted her to smile again.

The chirp of his phone took his focus away from Noelle. Checking the message, he read it, then said, "That's from Kyria. She's going to be late. Some decision about the house construction."

The smile he'd wanted to see on Noelle's face returned. "That's happened a lot lately. I was so happy when they moved here to Benton when Mark got the job at the hospital. I really like your sister. She's becoming a good friend. I wish we could spend more time together, but between my work and the boys, her starting her decorating business, and building their house finding that time has been tough. I get to see them at Hutch's or the Jenners' but not often enough. At church some, too."

Noelle took the tablecloth from him and moved to toss it in the large black bag lined garbage can. Turner saw a pile of bags with more tablecloths and opened one pulling the plastic sheet out. Together they began covering the table after she wiped it down with a wet rag.

"So, this event is a Harvest Hop? Not exactly sure what that is." Turner said. He had a general idea but figured the topic would lead to more conversation.

"The church holds it every year for the children of the church and the area. It's a way to do some outreach. Maybe get some families to see the reason behind Thanksgiving and Christmas rather than just pigging out and buying presents. There are games and races. Food, of course. A hay rack ride. They used to have an apple dunking, but too many kids got too wet doing it. A dance for the teens in the later part of the evening. Hutch gives a short talk about priorities and such. It's fun. My boys love the quarter hunt."

"Quarter hunt?"

"Yeah, they'll spread a couple of bales of hay out on the driveway and mix a few rolls of quarters in them, separated of course. Then the kids dive in and hunt for the quarters. They divide the kids up into age groups. They love it. Get all itchy with hay in their clothes, but my boys don't care."

She'd mentioned her boys several times. Was she

married? Turner glanced at her left hand. Her gloves were off as she worked with the slippery plastic. Her left hand had no rings, but when she reached to give him a corner he could see where a set had been, the indent was still faintly there.

Now he had a clue as to what the rough patch was. Noelle's marriage had broken up. Not that long ago either.

"You have boys? How many?" They spread the cloth on the table and began another.

"I have two boys, Camden who's six and in first grade and Mace who's four and in pre-school." She smiled as she told him, then it faded. "They're with their dad this weekend. I'm hoping he brings them tomorrow."

"You don't sound very optimistic about the prospect."

"I'm not. Ever since Phil decided his girlfriend was more in tune with his needs, he hasn't been real keen on going to church sponsored events."

Turner could empathize with that. He wasn't necessarily too interested in church events either, although with the pretty, young woman standing at the other end of the table smoothing the plastic tablecloth he just might enjoy one. Or more.

~~~~~

Noelle moved to the next table and tore the wrapping to release another table cover. There was a lot to do before the Harvest Hop tomorrow. Unfortunately, none of the rest of her committee had shown up to help. Not unusual. They knew she'd do it all so weren't very faithful in getting their responsibilities done. Then they'd show up for the accolades when the event went well. Seemed to be the story of her life. Doing everything and getting little credit for it, but all the blame if things went wrong.

She flipped the plastic cloth open across the table. The man who'd come to her 'rescue' grabbed it and helped straighten the orange plastic as it floated to the surface. He was broad shouldered, maybe a little over six feet. His black leather jacket looked to be tailored to exactly fit his body. There were pockets, both insert type and patch, on the front and sleeves. When he turned to walk to a different table, she thought there might be one on the center of the back. What could be in that one?

He had a biker physique, lean hips, and slim muscular legs. Light brown hair with streaks of blonde definitely reminded Noelle of his sister's. It was a bit longer than was popular at the moment and a bit on the shaggy side. It looked as if it was styled intentionally messy. There was a light beard, or maybe it was just that he hadn't shaved in a few days.

"That's the last of the tablecloths. What else needs to be done?" Turner asked.

Noelle pulled her focus from his shape and clothing, and they began setting up the serving table and coffee pots. They worked in silence for a bit.

"Hey," Noelle said. "I know I was a bit, um, distracted when you came in, but I didn't hear you drive up."

"That's because I didn't. I biked. Was just locking it when you screamed bloody murder."

The comment made her laugh. "I did, didn't I? I'm

pretty afraid of mice. Dirty, nasty creatures need to stay out of my path."

Turner joined her laughing.

"You really biked up here in this cold?" She placed the box of plastic spoons next to the one with forks.

"It's not that cold. Or at least it wasn't this afternoon. Kyria's going to take me back to her place. I don't like riding at night. That's why we were meeting here. I knew I wouldn't get back to her place until after dark. Glad we decided on that. I got to meet you, or should I say, rescue you from a gigantic rodent?"

"You're never going to let me live that down, are you?"

He grinned devilishly at her. "Most likely not."

"Well then, I might just have to put you to work tomorrow night, too. Looks like we've done all the damage we can tonight." They walked to the garage door, and she smacked the button to make it close. "Since Kyria's not here to pick you up how are you going to get to her place? It's dark."

"I was hoping you'd offer to haul me and my bike."

"I don't have a bike rack, and it's a small SUV."

He opened the man door and stepped back to allow her to precede him through. "It'll fit. It folds up pretty small."

Noelle watched as Turner unlocked the bike, pulled a couple of pins, undid some clamps and folded the lime green bike into the size of a spare tire. "That's pretty sweet. You can put it in just about any car trunk."

"Mostly. Doesn't fit in a Jag or Corvette trunk, among other small sports cars. I've tried. I do have a case so it can be checked luggage in when I fly. It's been all over the world with me."

Noelle was getting the idea that Turner just might be out of her economic status. Something about his casual attitude about traveling the world gave her a bit of a clue. She remembered Hutch saying Kyria was rather wealthy from an inheritance from her parents, and it seemed Turner was, too.

"I can give you a lift to Kyria's place, then." Noelle pressed the remote to unlock her car.

"Sweet. I'll text my sister and let her know she doesn't have to come get me." Turner pulled out his cell phone and spent some time pressing the keypad. The swoosh sound indicated delivery, then a few seconds later the phone chirped in reply. "She says great and that you can stay for supper. There's enough for you and the boys."

Turner opened the end gate and carefully laid the folded bike in the back. They got in and, after buckling the seat belts, Noelle started the car.

"Just me, but I'll take her up on the meal. Not often I get a home cooked meal I didn't cook or contribute heavily to."

Turner texted again, presumably to let Kyria know there would only be one more rather than three for supper. Then silence reigned as they wove through town.

"You mentioned work," Turner broke the quiet. "What and where?"

"I'm a nurse at the Benton Medical Center Urgent Care Clinic. It has regular hours and no swing shifts. Makes it easier as a single parent. I prefer hospital floor nursing but the twelve-hour shifts and odd weekends make it difficult. I switched to the clinic when Phil left."

They traveled the rest of the way in silence but not an uncomfortable one. That surprised her. Usually, when she first met someone any silence made her nervous. Sitting next to Turner didn't. It felt natural.

Soon they were turning into Kyria and Mark's driveway. They lived in a rental house they'd moved into when Mark took the head hospitalist job at Benton Medical Center a few months after their wedding. They'd begun planning their house then. Mark's family owned a construction company so it had jumped to the beginning of the list and was now enclosed and work would continue throughout the winter. They hoped to move in sometime in the spring.

Almost before Noelle put the car in park Turner was opening the door and jumping out. He got his bike out of the back and escorted Noelle to the front door. He didn't bother to knock, instead unlocked the door and went on in. That made Noelle nervous until she remembered he was living with them while he was in town.

"Hey, Kyria, Mark," Turner yelled as he placed his folded bike in the closet beside the door. "We're here." He took Noelle's coat and hung it up beside his.

Mark appeared in the doorway to what Noelle thought must be the kitchen. The foyer was only a tiled area in front of the door. There was a large living room with a white leather sofa, two blue upholstered chairs and a glass coffee table to the left. A large TV hung on the wall facing the couch. Light blue draperies hung on the large picture window. There were shelving units of dark brown wood flanking the window.

Noelle knew Kyria was an interior designer, but this room looked like it was a conglomeration of styles trying to fill the space. She was no whiz at decorating, but this just didn't quite work.

Her thoughts must have shown on her face because Mark laughed. "We just combined our furniture for now. Once the house gets finished some of our things will move to it and others won't continue as our possessions. We know it doesn't work well, but it's what we have. Kyria cringes every time she comes in here."

"It definitely doesn't do my career as a designer any good, so I don't bring clients here." Kyria entered wiping her hands on a tea towel. "So, you brought my wayward brother home, I see."

~~~~~

Mice and Marriage
A sweet Christian holiday romance coming Fall of 2017

www.ingramcontent.com/pod-product-compliance
Lightning Source LLC
Chambersburg PA
CBHW052002220626
47052CB00004B/1063